THE
MEALWORM
DIARIES

ANNA KERZ

ORCA BOOK PUBLISHERS

Library and Archives Canada Cataloguing in Publication

Kerz, Anna, 1947-
The mealworm diaries / written by Anna Kerz.

ISBN 978-1-55143-982-2

I. Title.
PS8621.E79M43 2009   jC813'.6   C2008-907305-3

Summary: Loss, grief and an annoying classmate
make Jeremy's adjustment to life in a new city
particularly difficult.

First published in the United States, 2009
Library of Congress Control Number: 2008940977

Orca Book Publishers gratefully acknowledges the support for its publishing
programs provided by the following agencies: the Government of Canada
through the Book Publishing Industry Development Program and the
Canada Council for the Arts, and the Province of British Columbia through
the BC Arts Council and the Book Publishing Tax Credit.

Design by Teresa Bubela
Drawings and hand lettering by Bruce Collins
Cover photography by Dreamstime
Typeset by Bruce Collins
Author photo by Frank Kerz

Orca Book Publishers
PO Box 5626, Stn. B
Victoria, BC Canada
V8R 6S4

Orca Book Publishers
PO Box 468
Custer, WA USA
98240-0468

www.orcabook.com
Printed and bound in Canada.
Printed on 100% PCW recycled paper.
12 11 10 09 • 4 3 2 1

To my students,
for making the workweek feel too short,
and to my family and all my friends
who kept saying "Yes, you can."

ONE

Jeremy gasped, his throat tight with the need to scream, as blood splattered his face and icy water washed over his body. His arms and legs thrashed as he struggled to escape. Then, gasping for air, he bolted into a sitting position. The room was dark, his bed soaked with sweat and…He groaned. *No. Not again.*

He knew he had to get up, change his pajamas and pull off the wet sheets before they got cold. He knew, but he wanted so much to slip back to the happy moment, the one that came before the bad part of the dream. He closed his eyes, reaching for it. There had been sunshine and wind from the sea, the smell of gas and leather, the sound of an engine roaring…and something…something else.

The hallway light sliced across his face, cutting off the dream images.

"Are you wet?" His mother's voice: soft, tired.

He squinted. "Yeah," he said.

He heard her cross the room and open a drawer. Something landed on his bed. Clean pajamas.

"Wash up and change. I'll take care of the sheets." She was already pulling off the quilt.

Jeremy slid out of bed and duck-walked to the bathroom, his flannel hockey pajamas dangling wet and heavy between his legs. When he came back, the sheets lay bundled by the door. He dropped his pajamas on top, walked over and climbed into bed.

"Same dream?" she asked, settling down beside him.

He nodded. "Was I screaming?"

"Just groaning a little. Do you want to tell me about it?" He heard the worry in her voice.

"I don't even remember," he said as he crossed his arms on his chest and tucked his hands into his armpits.

"Something happen today?" More of that worry. It was hiding behind the softness of her voice.

He shook his head, but when he looked up, he saw bracket lines form around her mouth. He couldn't fool her. He sighed and dropped his hands into his lap.

"Is it the new school? One of the kids? The teacher?"

"School's okay." He began making accordion folds with the edge of his blanket.

She waited.

"There's this guy in our class," he finally offered. "His name's Aaron. The kids call him Aaron Cantwait."

"What's his real name?"

"I dunno. He talks a lot. You know. Can't wait for his turn. He has to sit by himself at the front of the room."

"Anybody else?"

"I kinda made friends with the guy beside me. His name's Horace."

"Horse?"

Jeremy grimaced. "Not horse. Hor-ace."

"That's not a name you hear a lot."

"I guess. He's Chinese. There's kids from everywhere in this class."

"Big cities are like that. Anybody else?"

He shrugged. There was the girl who sat across from him. *Karima*, the nametag on her desk said. He had checked. And there was another boy, Tufan, who sat beside Karima in the fourth desk in their group. Tufan didn't talk much in class, but he talked plenty in the schoolyard.

"Left field, Shrimp," he had called to Jeremy when the boys set up teams at recess. Tufan was bigger than most of the kids in class, and he had that look that said he could be mean if he wanted to be.

Jeremy decided his mother didn't need to know about Tufan or Karima yet. "It was only the first day."

She nodded and he hoped she was done, but she went on. "What about the teacher? Mr. Collins?"

"He's okay. He's into science, big time. The whole room is filled with aquariums and things he calls *vivariums*. He has fish and turtles and a snake and a couple of frogs."

"He looked young," his mother said. She reached out to push a strand of hair off his forehead.

"He rides a bike—a bicycle," he hurried to clarify. "Horace and I saw him when he was locking it to the rack in front of the school. And he has this cool helmet. All black with flames on the sides. Horace said he's a dirt-bike racer."

His mother yawned, and that made Jeremy yawn too.

"Are you sorry you came?" she asked. "'Cause you know Nana and Grampa would take you in a flash."

"I'm not sorry," he said quickly. "I want to stay with you." He grabbed for her hand.

"All right." She smiled. "I hear you. Lie down now."

Jeremy stretched to give her a quick peck on the cheek before he slid under the quilt. His mother bent and kissed his forehead.

"Mom? I'm sorry I woke you. I'm okay. Really."

She stroked his cheek, then his hair, and he closed his eyes, enjoying the warmth of her fingers. Then she left, and he was alone, searching the dark behind his eyes, trying to find the filmy strands that might lead back to the happy part of his dream.

 TWO

"We're going to start a new unit today," Mr. Collins said as he picked up a blue plastic dishpan. "It'll give you a chance to do some scientific investigations."

"Is it gonna be a dishwashing unit? Is it a dishwashing unit?" Aaron was bouncing up and down in his chair.

Mr. Collins ignored him and went on. "As scientists, you will observe and record what you see in words and pictures."

"You mean like with a camera? Can we use a camera?" Same kid.

"Not with a camera, Aaron," Mr. Collins said. "Use your eyes and draw your own pictures."

"What're we gonna investigate?" Aaron again.

"*You* might want to investigate the art of listening," Mr. Collins said. "The rest of the class will study mealworms."

There were snickers. If Aaron heard, he didn't seem to care; he kept moving. His legs jiggled. He tapped his pencil on his desk. He hummed. His head bopped from side to side as if he was hearing music.

Weird kid, Jeremy thought.

Karima raised her hand. "Mr. Collins? What are mealworms?"

"Good question, Karima. Don't let the name fool you. They're worms, but they're not long or wet or slimy like garden worms. These are tiny, cute, little fellows."

Karima's nose wrinkled but she smiled, and Jeremy found himself studying the dimples that appeared in her cheeks.

"They're sold in pet shops as food for different kinds of reptiles," Mr. Collins went on. "You'll like them." He winked and Karima giggled. Then she turned to Jeremy, and he looked away, embarrassed to have been caught staring.

"I'm going to come around and introduce each of you to your own mealworm," Mr. Collins said. "Think of today as a 'get to know you' session. Choose a name for your mealworm, and while you're at it, think about any investigations you might use to find out as much as you can about them." He raised his voice a little as he added, "Keep in mind that this is a living creature and you don't want to do it any harm."

"I wanna dissect mine. Can I dissect mine?" Aaron called across the room.

"No, Aaron, you can't." Jeremy heard a sigh in the teacher's voice. That kid really was a pain.

Mr. Collins moved from one person to the next. At every desk he leaned down and cupped the student's hand in his own. When the hand lay open and relaxed, Mr. Collins reached into the bin and pulled out a little squiggly thing that he placed into the waiting palm. Everybody had a different reaction.

"Cool!"

"Ewww!"

"Gross!"

"It tickles!"

"I'm gonna hurl."

The teacher stayed, holding each hand until he was sure that the kid was going to be comfortable with the mealworm before he went to the next person.

"This little guy looks like he could use a friend," he said as he came to stand beside Jeremy.

Jeremy flinched. *Is he talking about me?* He looked up, relieved to see Mr. Collins waiting to hand him a mealworm. He opened his fingers and allowed the teacher to place the worm into his waiting palm. The mealworm whipped back and forth a few times before it lay still and Mr. Collins moved on.

The mealworm was small and kind of yellow—not even as long as Jeremy's little finger. It was thin and dry to the touch. Jeremy noticed that each time he moved his hand, the mealworm folded itself in half and whipped around again. After a bit it wriggled into a crack between two of his fingers and slid through. Jeremy caught it in his other hand. No problem. The mealworm didn't move all that fast.

"I'm going to call mine Superman," he heard Aaron say when Mr. Collins reached his desk. "Yeah, Superman!"

The teacher was speaking softly, waiting for what seemed a long time before he put a mealworm into Aaron's palm. He stayed, holding Aaron's hand for a while longer before he let go. Even then he didn't walk away.

Jeremy put his own mealworm down and leaned forward, his chin on his desk, and stared. He noticed a small brown dot, like a freckle, on his mealworm's body, just behind its head. "I'm gonna call you Spot," he whispered. The mealworm squirmed. Jeremy waited for it to lie still again, and then he blew on it gently. He noticed that the mealworm wriggled each time a breath of air hit its body.

His observations were interrupted when Aaron shouted, "Fly, Superman, fly." And before Mr. Collins could stop him, Aaron's hand whipped back and his mealworm came sailing across the room in a long arc. Without thinking, Jeremy reached up and caught it.

"Fly ball! You're out, Aaron!" Tufan called. Kids laughed and clapped.

"Great catch, Jeremy," Horace said.

Jeremy flushed. He glanced at Karima. She was smiling.

Aaron began making hyena noises as if what had happened was the funniest thing ever. He jumped up and down beside his desk; then he fell into his chair and rocked back and forth, clutching his belly as if it hurt.

"New score, Aaron," Mr. Collins said when the class was settled again. "Jeremy two, Aaron nothing."

Aaron looked confused. "What? What does that mean?"

"It means," Mr. Collins said, measuring out his words, "that you've tossed your mealworm away. Since Jeremy caught it, I think it's only fair that he keep it."

There was a howl of protest from Aaron and snickers from some of the kids, but Mr. Collins ignored them.

Jeremy reached out to corral the two mealworms that were now making their way toward opposite sides of his desk.

THREE

It wasn't fair. Mr. Collins had said, "I'd like you to work with a partner," and the next thing Jeremy knew, everybody was talking and pairing up. Jeremy turned toward Horace, but he was nodding at some other kid who had called, "Horace! Horace!" from across the room, and when he looked at Tufan, all he got was a frown.

A sick feeling settled into his stomach. Voices swirled around him, but not one of those voices spoke his name. He saw Karima look his way and felt his windpipe close. For one terrible second, he thought she might ask him to be her partner, but she turned to another girl just before he had to gasp for air. He wasn't sure if he was relieved or disappointed.

The classroom noises settled, and still nobody came to say, "Do you want to work with me?" They were all paired up.

Fine, Jeremy thought. *I don't care. I don't need a partner.* But even as he lifted his chin, he felt his shoulders droop. A prickly feeling at the back of his eyes forced him to blink. He took a deep breath and sat up. *I am not gonna cry. Not on the second day in this school. Not ever.*

He glanced up to find Mr. Collins watching. Would he say, "We're going to rethink the partners you've chosen"? Or something else…anything that would mean he wouldn't have to be the one left over.

Mr. Collins' gaze turned to Aaron. *Oh no. No. Not Aaron.* The teacher raised an eyebrow. "Well, Jeremy," he said, "you and Aaron seem to be the only people without partners. Since you're the keeper of Aaron's mealworm, you get to decide if you're willing to work with him or if you'd rather keep both worms and work alone."

There was a howl of protest from Aaron, but Mr. Collins kept his eyes on Jeremy, who was beginning to feel that everybody else was watching too.

"Loser," Tufan called out.

Jeremy's stomach clenched at the word, but it was Aaron who began to screech, "Am not! Am not!

Am not a loser! I'm smart. I'm smart! I'm smarter than you are!"

There were snickers.

"That's enough," Mr. Collins said firmly, and he frowned at Tufan. "I'll talk to you later," he said. Then he turned back to Jeremy.

"Well, Jeremy?" he asked.

Jeremy looked over at Aaron, who was now tapping his pencil against the edge of his desk. "Can...can I work alone?" Jeremy began. "Can I work alone if it turns out we don't work well together?"

"I can live with that," Mr. Collins said. "Can you, Aaron?"

Aaron shoved the eraser end of his pencil right up inside his nose and grinned like a gargoyle.

 FOUR

As it turned out, Aaron wasn't all *that* bad to work with. Not if you ignored the fact that he repeated everything he said, and if you didn't mind that he jiggled like a Jello boy. He never sat still. But he had ideas. He was full of ideas.

"Count the sections. Count them," he said, as he hovered over Jeremy. "How many are there? How many?"

"I don't know. More than ten. It's hard to tell," Jeremy said. "It moves all the time." *Just like you*, he thought.

Aaron bent down to see too, his nose so close to the mealworm it was almost touching. "Lookit his legs. Lookit his legs. Can you see them? Can you see them? Can you?"

"Not with your head in the way," Jeremy said. He was surprised when Aaron actually moved aside and gave him a chance to examine the mealworms with the magnifying glass. "I think there are six," he said.

"Six? Six legs? So it's an insect. It's an insect. Insects have six legs. Here. Lemme see." Aaron grabbed the magnifying glass.

Jeremy sucked in a mouthful of air. His fingers curled into fists. This kid was such a pain. In his old school, he'd never have worked with anybody like Aaron. He'd have told him to get lost, or drop dead, or...well, maybe not.

He remembered the time he'd threatened to punch out Charlie Hill because Charlie shouted, "Jer, Jer, the Teddy Bear," after him in the schoolyard. His father had chuckled when Jeremy complained at home.

"Life is easier if you ignore the dipsticks," he had said. So Jeremy did his best to ignore the teasing, and after a while Charlie got tired of calling him names and stopped. He sighed. Maybe he could ignore this kid too.

Aaron didn't make it easy. "It pooped. It pooped. Lookit. Lookit. See? My mealworm pooped right on your desk."

When Jeremy looked, there was a black spot in the middle of his desk, smaller than the period you'd put at the end of a sentence. Was it a mealworm dropping?

Other kids came over to examine the spot too, until Mr. Collins called out, "That's enough now. Let's get back to work."

But Jeremy heard, "Ewww. Right on his desk," and there were giggles.

After a while the teacher came around again, handing out small metal pudding tins, the lids peeled away. Each tin had a little bit of brown stuff at the bottom. "Bran," Mr. Collins explained.

"Can't they get out? Can't they get out?" Aaron asked.

"I don't think so," Mr. Collins said. "The sides are smooth and straight, and I'm hoping they'll like the food so much they won't try to escape. I'm not sure what the caretaker would say if we let an army of mealworms loose in the school."

A few of the girls said "Ewww!" all over again, but the boys chuckled.

Aaron huffed when Mr. Collins refused to give him a tin of his own. "It's up to your partner," he said, handing Jeremy two tins. "He's the keeper of your mealworm, remember?"

Then he raised his voice so the whole class could hear. "Use a marker to print your name and your mealworm's name on the side of the tin, and then tidy up and begin your journal entries."

Jeremy passed one tin to Aaron and printed the name *Spot* on the second. When he finished, he saw Karima wiping her desk with a couple of wet paper towels. She didn't say anything, but when she was done she handed them to Jeremy, so he wiped his own desk. He was happy to get rid of any mealworm poop, even if it was almost invisible. Tufan reached for the towels next, and then everybody got towels and followed their example. Jeremy felt better. Maybe his desk wasn't the only poopy one.

When Aaron left, Jeremy wrote everything he could think of in his mealworm diary, and he made a quick sketch of two mealworms sitting up as if they were having a conversation. One was wearing little square glasses; the other had a big letter *S* on his chest and a little cape across his shoulders.

Karima's laugh made him look up. "That's really good," she said.

He smiled and a warm feeling settled into his chest. There was something about her...was it her eyes? Whatever it was, it made all his Aaron troubles seem less important.

FIVE

"Man, it sucks to be you," Tufan said as they lined up for recess. "Aaron is such a creep."

Jeremy chuckled his agreement, but when he saw Aaron watching, not three feet away, he stopped. He didn't like the kid, but he didn't want to make fun of him either. To keep from saying anything else, he stepped to the side and knelt to retie his shoelaces as the line of kids swirled by him and out the door.

When he got outside, he found himself surrounded by a whole lot of kids he didn't know. He saw Karima looking at him and he turned away, afraid she might call him over. When he glanced back, she was unfolding a skipping rope. It wasn't long before he heard a familiar *slap, slap, slap* beating out the song she and her friends were singing as they skipped. He wondered how they'd feel if he asked to join them. He was good with the ropes, really good. But from what he could see, in this school skipping was only for girls.

There were other groups of kids nearby. Some were playing foot hockey. None of them were paying him any attention. At home somebody would have asked him to join in, or he would have walked over and said, "Can I play?" At home he never stood alone. At home he knew everybody.

He looked out into the field beyond the pavement and saw the boys from his class in the baseball diamond. By the way their arms were waving, he was sure they were arguing.

He'd found out yesterday that they played something called soccer baseball. Horace said real bats and balls weren't allowed in city schools, so they played a game with baseball rules, kicking a soccer ball instead of hitting a baseball with a bat. He waited to see if somebody would wave him over. Nobody did.

He turned, spotted the sign for the boys' washroom and thought about going in there. Would it be easier to hide in the washroom than to stand alone in a crowd? He shook his head, lifted his shoulders and headed for the diamond. He'd stand and watch if he had to. It was better than spending recess beside a urinal.

"Hey, Jer," Horace called as he came closer. "Where'd ya go, man? C'mon. We need you to make even teams."

To his surprise, Tufan yelled, "He's ours." And then, "Go play third base."

Jeremy smiled as he walked to his place. *That's all it takes to get a good spot on the team*, he thought. *One good mealworm rescue.*

It wasn't until the first kid was standing at the plate that Jeremy noticed Aaron. He was crawling on his hands and knees at the edge of the diamond, combing the grass with his fingers as if he was searching for something. Obviously he didn't play with the guys.

The game went fast. The boys kicked and caught and passed the ball easily. It was a good game, and Jeremy soon got into it. When he had a runner on third, waiting to race home, he watched the kid at the plate angle himself and he knew the ball would come his way. He got ready. The boy kicked hard, but instead of a long drive, the ball rose.

"I got it," Jeremy called, his eyes on the ball. He positioned himself, arms ready. It would be an easy catch. He stepped back, and back again, and swayed to correct his stance. There were shouts, but his whole body stayed focused on the falling ball. He raised his hands for the catch, took another step back and fell, his arms windmilling. He landed heavily on a body—Aaron's body—as the ball bounced into the dirt beside him.

There were cheers from the other team as three runners, one behind the other, crossed home plate, but his own teammates were hopping mad.

"No fair!" they shouted. "Interference!" And then, "Aaron! Aaron!" their voices loud with frustration and anger.

Horace came running. "You okay?"

"I didn't see him," Jeremy said, rubbing a sore spot on the back of his head. He checked his elbows. The right one was scraped and dust-covered, but there was no blood.

"Are you okay?" Horace asked again.

"Yeah. I'm all right."

The bell rang for the end of recess. Still arguing, the boys straggled off the field.

Jeremy stayed back. He wanted to say something, but didn't know what, so he watched Aaron sit up, push his glasses higher on his nose and look around.

Stunned, Jeremy thought. *The kid is stunned*. He kicked the toe of his shoe into the dirt. A small cloud of dust rose and drifted toward Aaron. *Too bad*, Jeremy thought. *Too bad for you*. Then he turned and ran to join the boys already lined up at the school doors.

SIX

"you up for a snack?" Milly asked, offering him a
e that held a couple of cheese slices, some apple
ges and a few crackers.

Jeremy looked up in surprise. He hadn't heard Milly
come outside, but he was happy to accept her offer of
food. "I'm always up for a snack," he said, accepting the
plate and placing it on the porch beside him. "My mom
says I have a hollow leg."

"My mother used to say that too," Milly chuckled.
"You have to wonder where that expression came from."
She turned and walked to the wicker rocking chair
beside the front door and straightened the flowery
cushion before she lowered herself down.

Milly was some kind of relative—his grandfather's cousin or second cousin, or something like that. He remembered his mother explaining it all when they were on the train coming to Toronto.

"Was she at the funeral?" he had asked.

"No. She sent a card," his mother said, and Jeremy had nodded and gone back to staring at the river and the trees and the telephone poles that flashed by his window. What he knew for sure was that Milly's husband was dead, her daughters grown up and gone. They were staying with her so his mother could go to college, and so there'd be someone at home for him after school or when his mother was at her part-time job at the grocery store.

Milly was a big woman, both tall and wide. She moved slowly and carefully, as if she was afraid she might step on something breakable.

"Welcome. Welcome. I'm glad you've come," she had said when they first arrived, and she had stretched out her hand to shake his as if he were a grown-up. "Call me Milly," she said. Jeremy had been relieved that she hadn't tried to hug him. He'd been hugged too often, by people he hardly knew. He decided that very first day that Milly was all right. She didn't try to boss him around or pepper him with questions.

They sat for a while, Milly rocking, Jeremy staring toward Queen Street where the streetcars ran, as if by watching he could make his mother come home earlier. Their pocket of silence seemed to amplify the noises of the city. There was a screech of tires, followed by the clang of a streetcar's bell and a horn, blaring. A siren wailed, paused as if to take a breath, then wailed again. The *whup, whup, whup* of a helicopter beat across the sky above them. Toronto was loud. Would he ever get used to the noises?

A couple of kids whipped by on rollerblades. He watched. It looked like fun. There had been no place to rollerblade where they lived in Nova Scotia. The side roads were dirt and gravel. Only the main roads were paved. But here? He thought about asking his mother for some, then decided not to. They weren't going to be here that long anyway.

"Autumn's coming," Milly said. "There's something in the air."

Jeremy nodded. He gazed toward Queen Street again. From his perch he could see cars flash by the end of their street. He wouldn't be able to see his mother get off a streetcar, but he'd know the minute she turned the corner and started toward the house.

He sat, watching the street so carefully that he didn't notice Thomas, Milly's ginger cat, until a cold nose probed his hand. Jeremy didn't move as Thomas folded himself into sitting position and settled down beside him. The cat sat so close that Jeremy could feel his warmth, and he reached over and began to scratch behind Thomas's ears. It wasn't long before the cat's body vibrated with a deep rumbling purr.

"He likes you," Milly said. "He's not always so friendly. Did you have a cat back home?"

"A dog," Jeremy said, but the catch in his throat stopped him from saying more.

He was with his father the day they found the dog. It was a blue and brown and golden day, just like this one. Was that only last year? No, it must have been two years ago now. He and his father had been walking along the riverbank, not talking, just walking. After an hour or so they stopped on a moss- and lichen-covered rock that jutted out over the water. His father settled on the ground and closed his eyes against the sun. Jeremy tied a line to a stick and baited his hook with a bug. Time and again he tossed it into the water, but if there were fish, they weren't biting.

For a while the only sounds were the water tumbling over stones and the short sharp call of a kingfisher. Then there was a new sound. His father sat up, scanning the riverside brush and small trees. The sounds came again from somewhere behind that, from the darkness of taller trees—grunting, whining, whimpering. Even now Jeremy remembered his fear: the tightness in his chest, his breath in his throat. *Bear?* They had passed some scat earlier.

"It's dry and old," his father had said. "Nothing to worry about. That bear's long gone."

But now Jeremy saw his father stand and tilt his head to listen. Then, without a word, he walked away through the dry grass, pushed through the shrubbery and the saplings and disappeared.

"Dad?"

No answer.

"Dad?" Panic filled Jeremy's mouth with a taste like metal. "DAD!"

"Jer? C'mere. Ya gotta see this."

Relief. It couldn't be a bear. He shoved his way through the undergrowth in the direction his father had taken. "Dad?"

"I'm here. C'mon."

Jeremy stepped into a clearing to find his father kneeling beside a cardboard box filled with four furry little bodies. Puppies. Not bears.

"Some people." His dad shook his head. "What kind of people dump puppies like garbage and leave them to die?"

The sight of the pups washed away Jeremy's fears, and he joined his father on the ground, letting the puppies clamber into his lap and lick his face. He remembered laughing as he petted, scratched and held the warm fuzzy bodies.

"Pick one. You can keep one," his father had said. So he had picked, but he had been sad when they had to leave the rest at the animal shelter.

His father had looked a little sad too, but he gave the peak of Jeremy's cap a sharp tug down and said, "You know we can't keep four dogs. They're healthy. They'll all find homes."

The girl behind the counter agreed, and Jeremy felt a little better.

"His name's Henry," he had told his mother when they showed her the squirming pup.

"Henry? What kind of name is that for a dog?" she had said, but the name stuck.

Beside him now, the cat stood and stretched elegantly, from his toes to his tail; then he leaped to the porch railing and tiptoed to the corner post where he sat, staring down the street, as if he was waiting too.

Jeremy turned to Milly. "My dog's name was Henry," he said. "We found him in the bush beside the river. Somebody dumped a whole litter and left them to die."

"Some people," Milly said, echoing his father's words.

SEVEN

"Today I want you to do some brainstorming," Mr. Collins told the class after recess. "You can use one page of your diary to make a list of possible mealworm experiments."

There was an excited buzz. Mr. Collins had to raise his voice to speak over the noise. "Don't forget," he called. "Don't do anything to harm the mealworms."

Kids popped out of chairs in their hurry to pair up. Only Jeremy took his time. He placed his notebook and pencil and both mealworm cans on his chair and dragged everything to Aaron's desk. When he arrived, Aaron walked away.

That's it, Jeremy fumed. *I've had it with this loser. I'm gonna work alone.* He looked around, ready to tell

29

Mr. Collins his decision. *I tried,* he'd say, *but I can't work with Aaron.* But Mr. Collins was across the room talking to some other kids, so Jeremy dragged everything back to his own desk and dropped into his chair. On the blank page in front of him, he wrote: *Mealworm Experiments.* He underlined the words so hard his pencil made a hole in his page. He sighed and tried to think about meal-worms. The first ideas came quickly, and he wrote:

1) *What colors do mealworms like?*
2) *How fast can mealworms travel?*
3) *What do mealworms like to eat?*
4)

What else? He stopped, chewed on the end of his pencil and looked around for inspiration. Across from him, Karima and another girl were adding to what already looked like a long list of ideas. Tufan was arguing with his partner, but even their list was longer than his. He saw Horace across the room. He and his partner were talking and waving their hands as if they were drawing their experiments in the air. Jeremy sighed. This would be fun if he were sharing it with a friend.

A grinding sound penetrated his bubble of silence. Aaron was at the pencil sharpener, his pencil now so short he was pushing it into the opening with the flat of his hand. He stopped and pulled the pencil stub from the sharpener.

"Mr. Collins. MR. COLLINS!" he called. "I need a new pencil. I NEED a NEW pencil."

Ha! Jeremy thought. *Mr. Collins will finally make him do some work.* He waited for the teacher to send Aaron back to his desk, but Mr. Collins barely looked up.

"Get some work done, Aaron," he said. "I'll get you a new pencil when I'm finished here."

If Aaron heard, he didn't listen. Jeremy saw him take the sharpener apart, empty the pencil shavings into the garbage can and twist the cover around until it clicked back into place. Even then he didn't come back to see what Jeremy was doing. He wandered to the other end of the room, stopped beside the snake's vivarium and moved his fingers across the glass. The snake inside rose and swayed, first left, then right, then back again, as if it was dancing to the movement of Aaron's hand.

A wave of anger rolled through Jeremy. *It's not fair,* he thought. *Why do I have to do this by myself?* He wanted to shout, "Stupid Aaron. Stupid teacher! Stupid school." He wanted to cry. No. Not cry. He didn't want to cry. When he looked up he saw Karima watching, her eyes soft and dark, and he took a long breath.

"Five minutes," Mr. Collins called.

That's when Aaron appeared. He put his elbows on Jeremy's desk, leaned into the middle of the experiment page and began to read in a voice like an announcer. **"Number one. What colors do mealworms like?"**

Tufan snickered. A hot flush rose in Jeremy's face. The urge to shove Aaron away became so strong that he had to clench his fists to keep his hands down. It didn't help that Aaron shook his head and said, "That's useless. Can't do that."

"Why not?" Jeremy asked, his voice tight.

"Mealworms. They're color blind. Your experiment's a dud. It's a dud. Waste of time."

"How do *you* know?"

"They're the larvae of darkling beetles, so that means they eat grain. Stuff like the bran Mr. Collins gave us to feed them."

"So?"

"So they're always in the *middle* of something or *under* something, where it's dark. Actually, they like the dark. They're nocturnal. They don't need to see colors, and nature doesn't give you what you don't need."

Jeremy stared. He was still mad, but the thought crossed his mind that, for a stupid kid, Aaron sounded pretty smart. "Larvae?" he finally said.

"Yeah. Mealworms are larvae. They're larvae. They'll metamorphosis, or something like that. They'll change. Into beetles. Like caterpillars change to butterflies."

"How do you know?"

"I know. I JUST KNOW." He gave Jeremy a twisted grin and crossed his eyes.

Jeremy frowned to let Aaron know he wasn't going to laugh.

"Actually," Aaron began, stretching the word so that it came out *ac...tu...al...ly*, before he went on in his regular Aaron voice, "I, I told my big brother we were gonna study mealworms, an' he took me to the library an' there was this book all about them. He, he even showed me how to find stuff on the Internet. It was way cool. Way cool! He knows everything like that. He's in high school. An' next Saturday he's gonna take me to the museum. He said. He said there's a whole case of darkling beetles there."

"Oh yeah? So what do *you* think we should do?"

"Let's, let's find out what else they eat. Like, we could bring some food from home and find out what they like. An' maybe we could find something dead, like a mouse. They might eat a mouse. Maybe. We could find out how far away they have to be to smell food. Like, we could make a maze. Yeah. A maze. An'...an'...an' we could see if they can find the food at the end. Like scientists always do with rats."

Jeremy stared. Aaron's hands were conducting his words, and he was keeping time with his feet as he spoke. He almost seemed to be dancing. *The guy was making sense, wasn't he?* Jeremy couldn't tell anymore. He felt as mesmerized as the snake in its vivarium.

"I like the maze idea," he said. "We can do the maze." And for the first time he was excited about this meal-worm study. On his page he wrote: *4) Can mealworms find food at the end of a maze?*

That's when Mr. Collins stopped the class. "Go through your list," he instructed, "and choose one of the experiments you'd like to try. We only have a little time left, so choose one that you can do in ten minutes or less. And remember to record your observations as you go along."

Jeremy looked over his list. "What do you think we should do?" he asked. There was no answer. Aaron seemed to have lost interest in mealworms and was on his knees, tracing tile lines with his finger. Jeremy's fist thumped his desk hard enough to make Karima and her partner jump. When they saw Aaron, Karima turned up her palms and shrugged as if to say, "That's Aaron for you." She smiled then, and Jeremy felt a little better.

He decided to try something easy so he wrote: *5) Do mealworms like the light or the dark?* It wouldn't be much of an experiment, but at least he'd find out if Aaron knew what he was talking about.

He covered one side of his desk with black construction paper, one side with white. Then he picked Spot and

Superman out of their tins and placed them in the bare space between the two pieces of paper. The mealworms whipped around, then stopped. Jeremy prodded Spot with the eraser end of his pencil. The mealworm wriggled as if in protest but didn't go anywhere. *Now what?*

From the other side of the room, he heard Mr. Collins call out, "Aaron, get back to work," and to Jeremy's relief, Aaron came back just as both mealworms started to move. The problem was that Superman slipped under the black paper and Spot under the white. It wasn't what Jeremy had expected.

"We've got one mealworm under each," he complained "What does that prove?"

"It proves, it proves what I already told you," Aaron said. "It proves mealworms don't like to lie around in the open." He tapped a finger on the desk to punctuate his words. "They like the dark, and they like to hide."

He frowned at the mealworms while Jeremy recorded their observations. Then he said, "I'm gonna change my mealworm's name. I'm gonna call him Darth Vader. Yeah. Darth Vader. 'Cause he likes the dark side."

This time Jeremy chuckled.

EIGHT

"…And from Mr. Collins…" The principal's voice came through the speaker for Friday's closing announcement. "Anyone in grade four, five or six interested in joining the cross-country team, please sign up with your teacher before leaving today. Meetings will be held every Monday and Wednesday at three thirty. If you are joining, please remind your parents you'll be home late on practice nights."

"Can I? Can I? Can I join?" Aaron called even before the announcements were done.

Jeremy heard groans from some of the kids, but Mr. Collins nodded. "I think running would be good for you," he said, and he wrote *Aaron* on the board.

Jeremy grinned. He wondered if the teacher wanted to write *Cantwait* beside the name.

"Anybody else?" Mr. Collins asked. Karima's hand went up, and the teacher added her name, looked around and kept writing when he saw other hands waving. He soon had a long list. Jeremy's name was on it.

"Just before you go," Mr. Collins called as the kids started to pack up, "take one of these papers home. They're order forms for new gym uniforms."

When Jeremy got his paper, he frowned. *It is important that all students change for gym class*, it said, and then it listed the clothing everybody could buy: socks, a T-shirt with the school logo, matching shorts. Shorts? Jeremy looked over the form a second time and then a third. Shorts. No way. He frowned and shoved the page to the very bottom of his backpack.

That night the dream came back. The happy part seemed to be shorter than ever, and Jeremy's heart soon boomed in his chest. He woke as the hallway light pierced his eyelids. He was gasping, his pajamas wet with sweat and... he groaned with embarrassment. His mother came over and wrapped her arms around his still-shaking body.

"Same dream?" she asked as she always did.

He nodded. "Sorry I woke you," he said. "Sorry." He gestured at the bedding.

"I wasn't sleeping," she said softly. "I've got an assignment due tomorrow. Tell me what happened today."

He thought about not answering. Thought about pretending he didn't know what was wrong, but there was no point. "There's a paper in my backpack."

His mother got up, lifted the backpack from its hook by the door and brought it over.

Jeremy unzipped the center section and rooted around inside. "You have to sign this," he said, pulling out the wadded paper.

She straightened the page and began to read. "It's because of the shorts?"

He nodded.

"Do you want me to talk to your teacher?"

"No!"

"He doesn't have to know everything," she said softly, "If you don't want me to talk to him, why don't you ask if he'd let you wear trackpants instead?"

Jeremy thought about that. "Maybe. D'ya think he would?"

"You said he's nice. Why wouldn't he?"

"Yeah. I guess."

They sat quietly for a while before his mother said, "You know, your scar isn't so bad anymore. It's not nearly as red as it used to be."

"It's ugly. Everybody will stare. They'll ask how I got it."

She nodded. "They probably will. Is it still too hard to answer?"

He shrugged. Then he whispered, "What if I cry?"

"What if you do? You're allowed, you know."

Jeremy's head dropped. His fingers worried a piece of loose skin around his thumbnail until his mother pointed to a sentence at the bottom of the order form. "It says here that the gym clothes won't be delivered for another three weeks. A lot can happen in three weeks."

He snorted. *Not enough,* he thought. Then he squirmed. The wet sheets were starting to cool.

His mother noticed. She patted his shoulder. "Go on, now," she said. "Go wash up. I'll change the bed."

He set the spray to come out of the showerhead hot and hard before he soaped a washcloth and scrubbed himself clean. The foam coursed down his legs. He watched it mound around his feet before it slipped down the drain. It wasn't until he was toweling himself dry that he took the time to examine his legs. He didn't like looking at them. The left one was fine. It looked almost like it always did, but that only made the right leg look worse. A red scar ran from the inside of his upper thigh, diagonally across and down over his kneecap, and from there it zigzagged down the outside of his leg to his ankle. He fingered its bumps and hollows and the knobby places where the screws and metal plates held the bones together. Was his mother right? Did it look better? Maybe the red didn't look as angry as it used to. No, he decided, it was still ugly. And there was no way he could hide it if he was wearing shorts.

Thomas's rumbling purr and the delicate tickle of cat whiskers on his cheek woke Jeremy in the morning. He knew that neither the sounds nor the tickling would allow for more sleep, so he sat up and pulled the cat into his lap. As he scratched Thomas, Jeremy's nose filled with the tantalizing aroma of bacon drifting up from the kitchen.

His mind flashed to another bacon morning. A morning when he woke to leafy shadows on tent walls, the sharp bite of wood smoke, sunshine wavering through tendrils of mist, a bird calling, and in the distance, water tumbling over rocks. There was laughter and the sound of his parents' voices. On that morning, it had been Henry's cold nose and wet tongue that had nudged him out of his sleeping bag. There'd never be another morning like it. He sighed.

He didn't want to get out of bed, but once his feet touched the floor, he dressed quickly and went downstairs. Milly was at the table drinking tea. When she saw him she smiled, stood up and handed him a plate of pancakes with bacon on the side. "Your Mom has the early shift at the store," she told him as she sat back down.

"Uh-huh." Jeremy's mouth was already filled with food. He chewed happily. "Great pancakes," he said between mouthfuls.

Milly smiled. "My mother's recipe. My girls loved them, and Fred always said they were the best he ever ate."

Jeremy nodded his agreement.

When he was done, he helped with the dishes. Milly washed, he dried. As they worked, she told him about Fred.

"You still miss him," he said as he dried the last dish and put it in the cupboard.

"Sure do. For a long time I missed him so much it hurt. It's better now though. And it helps to talk about him. Sort of feels as if part of him's still here, you know?"

Jeremy was silent, thinking about Milly's words. He understood what she was telling him, and the thought crossed his mind that Milly would be a good person to talk to. Probably she wouldn't cry like his mother did. Still, he wasn't ready to talk about his dad. Not yet. Maybe never. He stood with his back to the kitchen and took a long time hanging the damp towel on the stove handle. There *was* one question he wanted to ask. Did he dare?

"Well," Milly said, "that's that. I'm just going to sweep the floor. Why don't you go outside for a while?"

He took a deep breath. "Can I show you something first?"

"Sure," Milly said.

He pulled up his pant leg, but when the material bunched above his knees he frowned and let everything fall back into place. Frustrated, he looked up at Milly's puzzled face; then, with a small huffing sound, he fumbled to undo his pants and let them fall to the floor. It was embarrassing, but he'd dropped his pants for doctors and nurses so often over the last six months that it wasn't as hard as it used to be.

Milly eyebrows climbed up her forehead and almost disappeared under her hair.

"What do you think?" he asked.

Her mouth opened, closed, then opened again.

There, he thought. *It's so ugly she can't think what to say.* Then, to his surprise, she began to laugh, a deep warm chortle that made her body jiggle.

"You're...you're asking me about the happy-face boxers? I like them. They're cute."

"Not the underwear," Jeremy said, his voice tight.

"Oh," she said. "Oh." She sucked back her laughter. "What was it you wanted to know?"

"This! What do you think of this?" He lifted his leg and placed his right foot on a chair so she couldn't help seeing the scar.

He watched her smile fade as she examined his leg from top to bottom. "It's a humdinger, Jeremy. No doubt about that."

"It's ugly, isn't it?" he said, putting his leg back down.

"Ugly?" Milly took another long look. "I don't think it's as ugly as you think. It probably looks worse to you than it does to me. It's because you're looking at it from the inside as well as the outside."

"It's not ugly?"

"Well, it's not pretty, but no, it's not ugly either."

Jeremy examined her face. *Was she telling the truth? Was it only ugly to him?* He pulled up his pants, turning away to zip his fly.

When he was done, Milly smiled but she didn't say anything else. She went to the cupboard for the broom, and Jeremy went outside, the words *not ugly, not ugly*, replaying in his mind.

NINE

On Monday, Jeremy woke to the sound of rain drumming a steady rhythm on the roof. He knew, even before he opened his eyes, that this was going to be an all-day downpour, so he pulled the covers over his head and pretended that he could sleep a little longer.

Thomas didn't like that. He uncurled from his place at the foot of the bed, stretched and began kneading the mattress until Jeremy rolled over once, and then again, right out of bed.

"Jeremy!" It was Milly's voice.

"I'm up," he called, running his hand over the cat. Thomas stretched, twisted and raised one paw to begin a long slow cleaning of his fur.

Milly had a bowl of oatmeal waiting for him. "My Fred loved oatmeal on a rainy day," she said. "Do you want brown sugar or maple syrup on that?"

Jeremy gave her a sleepy smile and reached for the bowl of brown sugar. "My grampa likes oatmeal too," he told her. "Nana makes it for him every day. He always says, 'It's what a man needs to keep the plumbing in working order.'" The two of them chuckled, and then Jeremy ate until his bowl was empty. "What else did Fred like?" he asked when he was done.

"On cold days, he liked beef stew with lots of vegetables and potatoes," Milly said, with a dreamy expression on her face. "And he loved apple pies, the kind with the crumbly brown sugar and oatmeal topping."

Jeremy rested his head on his hand. An image of his dad standing by the old apple tree in their yard filled his mind. He could almost feel his father's arms hoisting him to a knobby branch, feel the leaves brush his arms. He watched himself reach for an apple, twist it free, pass it down. Saw his dad rub it against his pants until the whole apple gleamed. There was a loud crunch as he took a bite. Jeremy remembered the taste of the sweet-tart juice in his mouth when he took his own bite. He didn't try to tell Milly all that. "I like apples too," was all he said.

That morning Mr. Collins limped into class, his left arm in a sling. Some of the girls gasped. Karima's hand rose to cover her mouth.

"Don't worry," Mr. Collins said. "It looks worse than it is."

Kids began calling out questions, and Jeremy strained to listen but had trouble understanding the words through the thrumming that filled his ears. The sound washed in and out like ocean waves, breaking up Mr. Collins' voice. Jeremy heard, "…too fast…steep hill…wiped out…the bike's fine." There was relieved laughter.

Jeremy had to remind himself to breathe. He glanced at Karima. Saw her face mirroring her worry. Saw Aaron bouncing.

"Did…did…did you get hurt? Did you get stitches?" Aaron shouted. Jeremy's eyes went to the teacher's face.

Mr. Collins shook his head. "No stitches," he said. "No blood. Just a slight sprain and a lot of sore muscles. Now it only hurts when I breathe." He groaned then, and there was another burst of sympathetic laughter.

It rained all morning and through the afternoon, but Jeremy didn't mind that they had to stay inside. Mr. Collins had been teaching the class about chess, and Jeremy had really gotten into the game. He was sitting across from Horace, the two of them studying the board, when Aaron came by. They ignored him. He stood, silent, watching. Then Horace made a mistake, and Jeremy reached for his queen, expecting to make the winning move.

"Queen to rook four," Aaron said before Jeremy could put her down.

"No fair! No fair!" Horace complained, and Jeremy shouted Aaron's name in protest.

"But it's the right move," Aaron said.

"I know it's the right move," Jeremy said, "but now I can't make it. Thanks a lot. You just messed up our game."

"But—," Aaron began.

"No buts. Go away. Get lost. Butt out."

For once Aaron didn't argue. He looked confused, but he walked away. At the end of recess, Mr. Collins had to coax him out from under a table at the back of the room where he was rocking back and forth and talking to himself. Some kids snickered, and Tufan muttered something about "crazy." Jeremy had been thinking the same thing, but the word bothered him when he heard Tufan say it.

When it was still raining at three thirty, Jeremy expected all the after-school activities to be cancelled, so he was surprised to hear the principal announce, "Cross-country people please meet Mr. Collins at the gym doors."

Mr. Collins must have been surprised too, because he groaned loudly, and everybody laughed.

Jeremy was looking forward to running again. His leg ached a little on days as rainy as this one, but not too much, and as long as the new shorts were still on order, he could run in trackpants. He'd talk to Mr. Collins about the shorts once they arrived.

Horace led the way down the stairs and to the gym doors, where kids were milling about. It looked like more of a mob than a lineup. Jeremy heard a lot of talk and laughter and then, "Ewww! Look who's coming." That stopped him. *Are they talking about me?* He didn't have time to answer his own question, because somebody crashed into him from behind and sent him stumbling forward. More laughter.

He turned. *Watch where you're going,* was on his lips when he heard, "I didn't...I didn't..." It was Aaron, with Tufan standing right behind, looking smug.

"Hey, Cantwait," Tufan said, "I just *can't wait* to see you run." His words came with a mean laugh, and Jeremy heard stifled snickers from the crowd at the door. He almost felt sorry for Aaron.

One short sharp blast from a whistle cut through the hallway noise. "Line up," Mr. Collins called, and when everybody shuffled into a kind of line, he led the way into the gym.

A whole bunch of kids sat down with Tufan, but Jeremy didn't want to be in that crowd. He looked around, saw Karima sitting in a circle of girls. He couldn't join them, so he plopped down in an empty spot. Horace sat down beside him, and then Aaron came and squeezed himself into the space between them. *Too close, too close,* Jeremy wanted to say. Then he shook his head. He was starting to think the way Aaron talked.

I hope this guy isn't expecting to be friends, he thought as he glared at Aaron and shimmied to the left. Aaron didn't seem to notice. He was already busy unraveling the elastic from the top of his socks.

Mr. Collins limped to a chair and sat. Then he raised his right hand and waited for silence. "I checked out the

Farmer's Almanac," he began with a crooked grin. "You've heard of that, haven't you?"

The kids shook their heads. Jeremy wasn't surprised. Why would these city kids know what an almanac was?

"The forecast for September is rain, rain and more rain," Mr. Collins went on. "That's not good for the harvest and it's not good for cross-country runners, because it means that we're going to get wet and cold and muddy when we run." There were groans. "If you have a problem with that, you might as well forget about running and quit now." He looked around as if waiting for someone to get up and leave. "No? Well then, I can tell you that we're going to begin our training indoors."

There were relieved chuckles.

Mr. Collins divided the kids into teams. Jeremy found himself sitting last on a team with a bunch of girls and Aaron. *Great,* he thought, *I'm never gonna get away from this guy.* He decided that the only good thing about his team was that one of the girls was Karima. When he checked, he saw that the other teams all had more boys than girls, and the team Tufan was on was all boys. Jeremy's shoulders drooped. *It doesn't matter what we play, we're gonna lose this one.*

"Your job is simple," Mr. Collins began. "Run to the wall, pick up a skipping rope, take ten turns, then run back and tag the next person." There were a few groans from some of the boys, but everybody started shouting as soon as the first runners took off.

Jeremy was surprised at how fast the first girl in his team could run. She was small and skinny, but she really moved. When she began skipping, he started to cheer. On all the other teams, the first runners were boys, and not one of them knew how to skip. Their arms jerked the ropes up and over their heads and then smacked them hard to the floor. They pulled up their knees and jumped high enough to clear a fence, but the ropes tangled in their legs and slowed them down. By the time it was Aaron's turn, their team was actually ahead. "Go! Go! Go!" Jeremy shouted, excited at the possibility of a win.

Aaron took off, his neck stretched, his body bent so that the top was almost parallel with the floor, but his eyes were lifted to the ceiling. As he ran his toes pointed out to the sides and his feet made loud smacking noises when they hit the floor. His arms flapped with each step so that he looked like a wounded duck trying to take flight.

When he reached the skipping rope, Jeremy saw that all hope of winning was gone. Aaron couldn't bring it over his head. His arms rose, but the rope twisted in the air and his legs bent like pretzels every time he came down. Jeremy felt sorry for him all over again. He understood why Aaron chose to let the rope fall. Instead he bounced up and down on the spot ten times and headed back across the gym. There were calls of, "Cheater! Cheater!"; but Jeremy ignored them, and when Aaron tagged him he took off running.

The last runners on the other teams were already skipping when he reached his rope. Beside him, Tufan was huffing and muttering about "girly stuff" as he struggled to finish. Jeremy jumped twice. On his third jump he went as high as he could, stretched his legs forward and bent from the waist so that he seemed to be doing a sit-up in the air. Then he turned the rope fast. It whistled as it whipped around him four times before his feet came down, and then four more times on the next jump. When he was done he found himself racing back to his team behind Tufan. Last, but not dead last. There was a fine difference. He was prepared for more calls of "Cheater!" for not taking ten separate skips, but they didn't come, and when he looked up, Mr. Collins was looking back at him.

"Well, Jeremy," he said when the kids were quiet, "where'd you learn that?"

Jeremy paused. Should he tell? There didn't seem to be much choice. "I was on a skipping team back home," he said. Then he looked down.

"Are there other things you can do with a rope?" Mr. Collins asked.

"A few."

"I'd like to see some. Anybody else interested?" he asked.

Some of the kids began to clap, so Jeremy took the rope Mr. Collins handed him. He hadn't skipped in months. Not since before the accident. What tricks would his leg allow him to do? He began with simple heel-toe taps. They were enough to make people clap again, giving him the courage to go on. He folded his arms back and forth to do cross-overs. They were harder. He felt his bad leg tiring. Should he stop?

"Way cool!" A voice called out. It was enough encouragement to make him decide to try his very best trick.

Jumping at a steady pace, he went faster, then lifted his arms and let the rope fly up. As it rose, he kept his feet moving until it dropped again, into his waiting hands. He skipped for a few more beats, then trapped the rope under his raised toes and stopped.

There was a long moment of silence, filled only with the short sharp gasps of Jeremy's breath, until Aaron's voice called out, "Go, Skipper, go!" Then there was laughter and more applause, and Jeremy felt good.

On his way out of the gym with all the other kids, he was bodychecked into the wall. It happened fast—

too fast to see who did it. It might have been an accident except he was sure that he heard someone say "Suck-up" just before he was pushed. He thought he recognized the voice, but he wasn't sure until recess the next day, when Tufan pointed to right field and said, "Skip out there and try not to trip."

TEN

On Friday night Jeremy lay in bed, his hands behind his head. His eyes followed the finger-like shadows of tree branches that slid across his ceiling and down his walls. It was hard to sleep in the city. For one thing, his bedroom never got completely dark, and even with the curtains pulled, streetlights and porch lights and the probing beams of passing cars brightened the room. From Queen Street came the sounds of traffic: the *clickity-clack* of streetcars, the rumble of a passing truck, the occasional squeal of tires, the blare of a horn. The house was silent. Not even TV voices drifted up the stairs. Milly must be reading. He turned and snuggled into his quilt as the shadows danced on.

"Don't wait up," his mother had said. "I have to stay late for the store inventory." But he wouldn't sleep. Not until he knew she was home, and safe.

The front door opened and closed. A murmur of voices. He waited, expecting his mother's steps on the stairs. She always checked on him before she went to bed. Instead he heard the click of cups on the table. The shrill whistle from the kettle. They were going to have tea.

Unwilling to sleep, he slipped out of bed and padded across the room and into the hallway. His mother's voice drifted up from the kitchen: soft, sad, tired. He tiptoed to the landing and sat on the top stair in time to hear Milly say, "...in bed for a couple of hours."

For a while the only sound was the clink of a spoon in a cup. That had to be his mother. She always stirred and stirred her tea. His father used to tease that she couldn't drink before the spoon was worn out and cried uncle.

Finally there was a soft murmur of voices. At first he couldn't make them out. Then he heard his mother say, "Dan loved cars," and later, "...but I quit school and we got married."

They talked for a while, about Nova Scotia, about his grandparents. Jeremy yawned and thought about going back up to bed. Milly's words stopped him. "He worries about you," she said.

"I know. He never used to. But..." There was the sound of a stifled sob. It was enough to make Jeremy's stomach cramp. He folded his arms across his middle and leaned his head against the railing.

"Sorry," he heard his mother say. She blew her nose. "It's been...It's been a bad day. Back home I thought about Dan all the time. I thought it might be a little easier here. It is, I guess. Until today." There was another long silence. "It's kind of an anniversary. Fourteen years ago today Dan and I went on our first date. And now... It all happened so fast."

Jeremy groaned. *She's going to tell,* he thought. *She's going to tell.* He was afraid of what was coming. He didn't want to hear, but he couldn't stop listening.

"It was near the end of March," she said. "We'd had a few warm days. The ground was still frozen, but most of the snow had melted. There were puddles on the road. Jeremy had a practice to go to. His skipping team was going to perform for some provincial group. Gym teachers, I think. Doesn't matter."

Silence.

Jeremy could almost hear her take a breath before she went on.

"Anyway, Jeremy was out front, waiting. Dan was supposed to come home early to take him, but he was late."

I was playing with Henry.

Jeremy remembered tossing the Frisbee, the dog sprinting back and forth, leaping to catch the flying disc, until they were interrupted by the sounds of a motorcycle turning into the driveway.

"It was bad enough that he was late"—his mother's voice was louder now—"but he showed up on a motorcycle. One of the guys he worked with had this big black Harley. Dan thought he'd give Jeremy a thrill and ride him to his practice on it."

Jeremy could picture his father tugging off the helmet, smiling, shaking his head, running his fingers through his tousled hair. "Know anybody who wants a ride?" he had said.

"Jeremy!" He remembered the sound of his mother's voice from behind the screen door. Short. Sharp. Angry. "Put the dog in the run," she called, and he knew what else she was going to say. *She was going to say no. She was going to say I couldn't go.*

"Aw, Mom! Please?"

His father's face, hard now, the smile gone. "Do what your mother says."

He ran to the back, Henry bounding beside him. The dog still wanted to play. Didn't want to be locked up. Jeremy had to go into the run first, coaxing Henry to follow. Then Jeremy squeezed out, leaving the dog behind.

"And he only had one helmet," his mother was saying, the words sounding raw as they came out of her throat. "'You can't take him without a helmet!' I was yelling. I was furious with him."

Jeremy stood, an angry shiver coursing through his body. *You shouldn't have yelled*, he wanted to tell her. *That's why he gave me the helmet. He gave it to me. He should have been wearing it.*

"He shoved that huge helmet right over Jeremy's head. It was way too big and too heavy. It sat on his shoulders and wobbled. Jeremy could hardly see."

I could so. I saw. I saw everything.

He heard his mother sob. The sound made his knees buckle, and he slumped to the stairs.

"It seemed like they were hardly gone before I heard the first sirens, and I thought, 'No. Can't be.' And after a while there were more of them, wailing past the house, and it was like I knew. I knew. I was already outside, running up the driveway when Officer McKendrick pulled in." Her words burst out between more sobs. "I thought...I thought both..."

Jeremy's hands slipped over his ears. *Stop! Stop crying! Stop crying!*

It was a while before she spoke again, and this time her words were muffled by his hands. "They took me... Jeremy's leg was...operation...two metal plates...He missed the funeral. People came to see him. He wouldn't talk to anybody."

They were crying. They cried and felt sorry for me. *They felt sorry for* me. *I hated that they felt sorry for me.*

"He won't talk about it." She blew her nose again. It was a while before she went on. "...some nights... terrible dream..."

There was a soft murmur from Milly.

"I don't know...something triggers them...wets the bed...the doctors...something about the accident. Something he hasn't talked about. He could tell me. He could tell me anything. Why doesn't he tell me?" She cried again.

Jeremy slumped against the railing. *Can I tell her? Not this. She'll...*

He heard Milly make comforting noises and after a while the crying stopped. The sound of chairs scraping and cups clinking brought him to his feet. He was under the quilt with his eyes closed when his mother came in. He heard her soft footsteps, felt her breath warm on his face, her lips on his forehead. More steps. Only the shadows and his memories stayed.

ELEVEN

This will be perfect, Jeremy told himself as he walked with his mother to the streetcar stop. She had a day off. The sun was shining, and they were going to spend the time together. At the corner she pulled two streetcar tokens from her purse and slipped them between her lips to hold them as she fumbled to close the clasp.

"Milly says the Queen car runs across the whole city," she said, her voice high and thin as it came from the side of her mouth. "We can go anywhere."

"Anywhere?" Jeremy squeaked back, and his mother hurried to take the tokens from her lips. She laughed then, and Jeremy laughed too, and something lifted from his chest. He felt good.

"We could get off at Yonge Street and walk up to that big shopping mall Milly was telling us about. The Eaton Centre?" She passed him a token. "Or we could go all the way to the other end of the city and see High Park. We could spend the afternoon there. We have time to decide. Let's make it an adventure." She smiled.

When the streetcar came, he got on first and led the way to the back, where he settled on the bench seat. He liked this spot. He could look out through the center aisle and watch people get on, or he could turn and see what he was leaving behind.

The streetcar rumbled and bounced along, picking up passengers at every stop. There were old ladies clutching purses; women with plastic shopping bags; students with backpacks; moms with little kids clutching their hands; old men with tired eyes; and teenagers with headphones plugged into their ears, their heads moving to an unheard beat. Most of them got on in silence, scanned the car for a seat, swung into an empty spot and then stared out the window.

It was a quiet ride until a bunch of bigger kids streamed on, laughing, joking, jostling, shoving each other in a friendly sort of way. A couple of the girls dropped into seats near the front, but all the others stood, straddling the aisle to keep their balance as the streetcar rocked along. Some of the passengers glanced

at the noisy group, then looked away. Jeremy didn't think
that these city kids looked any different than the teenagers back home. They wore jeans with tattered hems
that trailed threads and T-shirts covered with words, or
pictures, or both.

At the next stop the driver called, "Clear the doors,"
and a few of the kids drifted toward the back, but they
kept calling to each other. Then, out of the jumble of
voices, Jeremy heard, "...and after the mealworms...
after the mealworms, can we see the mummy? I want
to see the mummy."

He cringed. Aaron? Yes. There, beside a tall boy
who was gripping the upper rail with one hand. His
other hand was on Aaron's shoulder as if to keep him
grounded. Aaron had said he was going to the museum
with his brother. This had to be him.

Jeremy slid lower in his seat. Between the bodies of
the passengers, he stared at the tall boy. He was wearing
a black T-shirt with the image of a gleaming motorcycle, the rider crouched, his head forward, his hands
clutching the grips. *A Harley*, Jeremy thought. The rider's
helmet was black and shiny, the visor down. Only his
green eagle-eyes showed.

"Dad's eyes were brown, weren't they?" he said.

"Yes," his mother said.

He jumped. He hadn't realized he had spoken aloud.

"This is Yonge Street coming up," she said. "If we're going to shop at the Eaton Centre we have to get off now."

"Let's just go on," he mumbled.

"Can we see the dinosaurs too? I love the dinosaurs." Aaron's voice carried through the streetcar. The tall boy smiled down at him with that happy but tired smile people use with a barking puppy. When he leaned down and said something to Aaron, Jeremy noticed a metallic gleam in his mouth—a silver stud buried on his tongue. Without thinking, Jeremy lifted his hand to cover his own mouth.

The movement must have caught Aaron's attention because he stretched his neck and peered toward the back. "Hey, Jeremy!" He called and waved as he wove his way between passengers. "I'm going to the museum with my big brother. We're gonna see the mealworms and the darkling beetles. Yeah. And the mummy, even."

"Tell everybody, why don'tcha," somebody called, and there was laughter.

The boy with the motorcycle shirt trailed Aaron to the back. "This is Jeremy," Aaron said loudly enough for everyone to hear. "He's my friend."

"Hi, Jeremy," several voices called.

Jeremy squirmed at the laughter that followed.

The tall boy finally caught up. He smiled and said, "I'm Paul. Aaron's Big Brother. I get to take him out once every two weeks. He can always think of some place he wants to go on our days together."

Jeremy's mother smiled back. "It's nice to meet you, Paul. You too, Aaron," she said. Then to Jeremy, "The museum's a great idea. Would you like to go?"

"Not today," he said quickly.

"It's pretty neat," the tall boy said. "Go if you get the chance."

"It's way neat. Way neat. It's got everything." Aaron nodded.

"University! University Avenue," the driver called.

"That's us. C'mon, Aaron. Let's roll."

When the tall boy turned, Jeremy could see the back of his shirt—a motorcycle leaving, trailed by a funnel cloud.

"There's even totem poles," Aaron called before he stepped down into the street.

"So that's Aaron," his mother said with a grin.

"Now you know why he's called Aaron Cantwait. And just so you know, we're not friends or anything," he added.

From the rear window, Jeremy watched the group on the sidewalk, a heaving shifting mob with Aaron bouncing in the middle.

 TWELVE

High Park was filled with people—moms and dads and kids, grandparents on lawn chairs and babies in strollers. Some people had pulled together two and three picnic tables and raised canopies to keep off the sun. They had portable barbecues and coolers. Some had covered the weathered tables with brightly patterned tablecloths. All of them seemed to be talking and laughing. They looked happy.

"It's nice here," his mother said.

"Hmmm." Jeremy nodded. It was nice. *But it's not home*, he thought. *Not enough trees, not enough water. And people—so many people—all of them strangers.* He yearned to be home in his corner of Nova Scotia where he knew everybody. Where everybody knew him.

He glanced at his mother and saw his sadness reflected in her face. That only made him feel worse. He looked around for something to cheer her up. Then he saw it. "Look," he said, pointing to a green dragon kite with a rainbow tail that hovered above a tree across from them. "See it? Right up there."

His mother smiled, and Jeremy did too as they watched the kite float on the wind. They saw it jerk sharply, first left, then right, and then it spiraled down.

"Oh! It's going to get snagged," his mother said. She was right. The kite dropped to a branch and hung with its dragon's head on one side, the tail on the other. On the ground below, the small boy clutching the string started to cry.

"Poor little guy," Jeremy's mother said.

She began to rummage in her bag, but Jeremy's gaze stayed on the boy and the kite. He saw a man hurry across the grass and put his hand on the boy's head. The man wiped the boy's nose with a tissue before he scrambled up the trunk and hoisted himself into the tree.

"Jeremy," his mother said, "there's something we have to discuss."

Jeremy heard, but he wasn't listening. He was watching the man in the tree belly-crawl along the branch and stretch out his arm. The man tugged on the kite string, pulling gently, this way and that, until the kite floated free, right down into the waiting arms of the boy.

An unexpected wave of feeling hit Jeremy. The muscles in his face stretched, his jaw tightened and he found himself blinking away tears that stung the back of his eyes.

"Oh, Jeremy!" his mother said. "We don't have to go."

"What?" He recognized the sound of worry. "What?" he said again.

"We can stay with Milly. She's invited her daughters and their families, and she said we're welcome to join them. So if you'd rather stay here, we don't have to go home for Thanksgiving. Nana and Grampa will understand."

"Thanksgiving?" Jeremy stared at his mother. *What was she talking about?*

"Nana phoned last night and asked if we wanted to come. We could leave a couple of days early and make a small holiday of it. We won't have time for another one until Christmas. I thought I'd ask you before I said yes. But we don't have to go. We can stay here if you'd rather."

A peacock's haunting cry drifted up from the animal pens at the edge of the park. "No," he said, "I want to go. I do." He wasn't sure if that was true, but he thought it was what his mother wanted to hear.

THIRTEEN

"I do not! I do not!" Aaron's shrill voice rang out as Jeremy and Horace rounded the corner of the school. They almost bumped into Tufan. The bigger boy was towering over Aaron, one hand on the wall above Aaron's head, his face spitting close.

"I do not. I do not," Tufan mimicked in a screechy voice.

"I do not!" Aaron shouted again, but his voice cracked with frustration, and Tufan laughed.

This doesn't look good, Jeremy thought, but he wasn't sure what to do about it.

"Come on," Horace said. "It's none of our business."

Jeremy hesitated before he followed. "Wonder what Aaron did this time?"

Horace shrugged. "Who knows. Aaron can piss anybody off just by looking at them."

"Jer? Jer-e-my?"

Jeremy looked back. The pleading look on Aaron's face stopped him.

"I-I wanna play. I wanna play soccer baseball," Aaron called. "Tell him to let me. Tell him."

"I-I-I don't think so!" Tufan mimicked. "We're not having any bed pizzers on our team. Not one."

A sharp pain twisted in Jeremy's belly.

"I told you I don't. I don't! I don't!" Aaron's voice rose until his words turned into a painfully high-pitched howl that made Tufan step back.

"Shut up," he growled. "Shut up before a teacher hears."

"Too late for that," Mr. Collins said as he stepped around the corner of the school. "What's going on?"

Tufan twirled his finger beside his head and smiled a twisted smile. "I dunno. This guy's just plain crazy."

"Try again, Tufan," Mr. Collins said.

"Nothing's going on, really. We were just talking about soccer baseball. Right, Jeremy?"

Startled to be included, Jeremy looked at Tufan and then back at the teacher.

"We just got here," Horace jumped in.

"Aaron?" Mr. Collins said.

Aaron had stopped screaming when the teacher arrived, but now he began banging his body against the wall in a steady beat that had to hurt.

Mr. Collins walked over and put a hand on Aaron's shoulder. "Aaron," he said firmly. "Stand still and tell me what's going on."

Aaron shuddered and closed his eyes, but he stopped the body-banging.

Jeremy expected Aaron to be silent after all that. Probably Tufan did too, because he looked surprised when Aaron said, "I wanna play soccer baseball with the other guys." Then he pointed at Tufan and shouted, "And he says I can't! Tell him I can play!"

"He can't. Tufan jumped in. "It's not because we don't want him to play," he went on smoothly. "He just can't. He can't catch a ball or throw it, and he can't kick for beans. Besides, when we let him play all he does is crawl on the ground and pick grass. People trip over him. Isn't that right, Jeremy? You tripped over him. He's such a loser. Nobody wants him on their team."

Mr. Collins frowned at Tufan before he looked at Aaron. For a long moment he didn't say anything. "I can see the problem, Aaron," Mr. Collins finally began. "Games aren't much fun for the rest of the guys if you can't stay focused."

Aaron looked down to where the toe of his shoe was trying to poke a hole in the pavement.

"But there might be a couple of things we can do," Mr. Collins went on.

That got everybody's attention.

"If you're keen to learn, Aaron, we could spend a few minutes of each gym class practicing how to throw and catch a ball."

Tufan groaned and Aaron's shoulders drooped.

"It's a beginning," Mr. Collins said to Aaron, trying to sound cheerful. "And we could pair you up with a buddy or two at recess." He looked hopefully at Horace and Jeremy, but they glanced at each other and looked away. "Throwing and catching are not things you can learn in one lesson. It takes time, but if you're willing to work at it…" Aaron's head was still down. "What about home?" Mr. Collins went on. "Is there anyone at home who could help?"

"Maybe. Maybe my big brother," Aaron said, his voice a low mumble until he added, "He's good at stuff like that."

"He doesn't *have* a big brother!" Tufan sputtered. He had been frowning since Mr. Collins suggested that the class might spend gym periods practicing how to throw and catch a ball. "He doesn't have *any* brothers, not big or little. He doesn't even have a dad or a mom.

He lives with his *grandmother*," he said, making the word *grandmother* sound pathetic.

"I do so!" Aaron shrieked. "I do so. Everybody has a mother and father or they wouldn't be born."

"That's enough, Tufan," Mr. Collins warned.

"He has a big brother," Jeremy piped up. "I saw him." He might have said more, but a look from Tufan silenced him.

The school buzzer signaled the end of the lunch break. "We're not done with this," Mr. Collins said. "I want to talk to the four of you after school." He rang the handbell.

"After school?" Horace began as soon as Mr. Collins stopped ringing the bell. "But sir, we didn't do anything."

"I noticed that, Horace. You didn't do a thing." He clanged the bell again, and with one hand still on Aaron's shoulder, he led the way to the doors.

"What did that mean?" Horace grumbled under his breath as he and Jeremy followed.

"I guess it means we were supposed to help Aaron," Jeremy muttered, but he was annoyed. *Why should Aaron be my problem?* he thought. *I didn't ask to be his partner. I'm not his friend. Why should I come to his rescue every time he gets himself in trouble?*

A heavy bump from behind sent him lurching forward as Tufan barreled past, then deked into line ahead of him. "You just remember whose side you're on," Tufan snarled over his shoulder.

"I'm not on anybody's side," Jeremy said, furious now. "Besides, it's your fault Aaron went nuts and started screaming. Why'd ya have to call him a bed pizzer?"

"'Cause he is. You can tell from the smell. It's that 'oh de pee.' It stays with them." Tufan snorted as he hurried into the school with Horace right behind him.

The words stopped Jeremy cold. *Can he smell me too? Can everybody?*

"Jeremy?" It was Mr. Collins' voice. "You coming?" He was holding the door, waiting. Jeremy hurried through.

They started down the hall together, but Jeremy fell back. *Can he smell me? Is that why he thinks I should be Aaron's friend?*

His stomach began to churn and his breath felt tight in his chest. "Can I go to the bathroom?" he gasped.

"Sure," Mr. Collins said. "Are you all right?"

"Yeah," Jeremy called back as he rushed into the boys' washroom. Once inside, he stopped. He heard the door *shush* and close with a hollow *thud*. The room sounded empty, but he bent down and checked for feet in the cubicles. There weren't any.

When he stood up he stared at his reflection in the mirror, grimaced, then squatted again and tried to put his nose as close to his crotch as he could. He sniffed several long slow breaths. Nothing. Maybe a faint smell of laundry detergent, but that was all. There was no other smell. He was sure.

He straightened, thinking of the times Aaron had worked beside him. There had been no smell then either. He would have noticed. He stared into the mirror again before he clenched his teeth. *That Tufan. He's just full of it.*

FOURTEEN

When it came to trouble, Jeremy could see that this city school was no different than his school at home in Nova Scotia. By the time he walked into the room, the whole class knew what had happened in the schoolyard, and they were all waiting to find out what Mr. Collins was going to do about it. For most of the afternoon, Jeremy kept his head down and his eyes on his work, but that was because he didn't want to see the curious looks from the other kids. As far as he was concerned, the whispers he heard were embarrassing enough. He didn't like being in trouble and he didn't think he and Horace were being treated fairly. *We were minding our own business*, he kept telling himself. *We didn't do anything wrong. Why should we be responsible for Aaron?*

It was almost three thirty before Mr. Collins called to the boys and motioned for them to come and stand by his desk. They shuffled to the front and stood in a restless row as the rest of the class watched. Mr. Collins turned to his computer, typed, then tapped an impatient finger while the machine whirred and hummed.

Other noises came from Aaron. Jeremy glanced over and saw him sucking on the cuff of his sweatshirt. Wet, straggly threads already dangled from his wrist. If the teacher didn't say something soon, there wouldn't be much cuff left. The final bell rang as Mr. Collins swung his chair around to face the class.

"Hold on!" he called, to stop everybody from packing up. "There's something I want to tell all of you before you leave. I've been doing some research about skipping, and I think it's something we could try."

He ignored the groans that came from the boys as he went on. "What I'd like is for the four of you"—he nodded at the boys beside his desk—"and anybody else that's interested, to work together to come up with a skipping routine that we could use for our next assembly. I think it would be a good way to introduce the new gym uniforms to the school."

"I'm not skipping," Tufan sputtered. "Skipping's for girls."

There were snickers from the class, and Jeremy felt his face get warm, but the laughter stopped when Mr. Collins raised an eyebrow and frowned at Tufan.

He turned back to his computer, hit some keys and turned the screen so everybody could see a picture of a large man, sweat dripping from his face and chest. In his hands you could see the handles and around him the blur of a rope. It was clear that the man was skipping.

"Muhammad Ali, former World Heavyweight Champion boxer," Mr. Collins said with a grin.

"Yeah but…," Tufan started.

The teacher raised a hand to quiet him and pressed another key. There was a picture of a line of boys jumping through a long rope, and that was followed by pictures of more boys doing cartwheels and push-ups in skipping ropes.

"I'm not expecting you to do anything like this by next week," he said with a grin, "but I thought we might be able to work out a simple routine. He looked toward Jeremy. "What do you think? Can you turn these three guys and some of the rest of the class into skippers in time?"

Jeremy's jaw dropped. "Me?"

"It's too hard," Tufan growled. And Jeremy, remembering Aaron's duck-run across the gym, nodded.

"It's girl stuff. You said so yourself," Mr. Collins grinned at Tufan. "How hard can it be?"

Ignoring all protests, he turned to the rest of the class. "We'll start after school today. Who else wants to join a skipping group?"

A few hands popped up, mostly girls, but there were a couple of boys. Jeremy noticed that some kids were smiling, and one of those kids was Karima.

"Well?" said Mr. Collins to Jeremy.

Jeremy shrugged. "Maybe. I guess."

In the gym Mr. Collins handed out skipping ropes. "All right," he said, "let's see what you can do."

Kids began jumping. The girls were pretty good. The boys weren't, but everybody tried, even Tufan.

Mr. Collins watched for a few minutes before he walked to a CD player and turned on some music. He moved his head to the loud steady beat, then picked up a rope and began skipping. That stopped everybody. Mr. Collins was fast, and he did some pretty smooth footwork. The sight made Jeremy sigh in relief. The teacher obviously knew what he was doing. Maybe a demonstration assembly was a possibility after all.

Now all he had to worry about were the shorts. He could hardly ask to wear trackpants for an assembly that was supposed to introduce the new gym uniform. But was he ready to wear shorts?

FIFTEEN

Loud talk and excited laughter filled the hallway beside the change-room door as the line of kids jostled back and forth. They were dressed in the new blue shorts and white T-shirts as they waited to perform the skipping routine Jeremy and Mr. Collins had helped them put together for the morning assembly. It was Horace who noticed that Jeremy was missing.

"C'mon, Jer," he called into the change room. "What's taking you so long?"

Jeremy jumped when he heard his name; then he sighed and stood up. He had been slumped on the bench, trying to gather his courage to take off his trackpants.

It's not pretty, but it's not ugly either, Milly had said. He hoped she knew what she was talking about.

On the floor in front of him, Aaron sat, struggling to make the loops on his shoelaces come out even. He looked up in time to see Jeremy shuck off his pants, so he was the first to see the red line that zigzagged down Jeremy's leg.

"Oh man! **Oh man! OH MAN!**" he said, his voice rising with each word. Everybody heard.

A tight band snapped across Jeremy's chest, and he sagged to the bench as boys drifted back into the room and girls clustered in the open doorway. He glanced down. The scar seemed redder and longer and uglier than ever. *Gross! Gross! Gross!* The words screamed in his head. He looked up at their faces. Saw their surprise. Heard their exclamations.

"Holy cow!"

"Man, that had to hurt!"

Then the questions started.

"What happened?"

"Was it a car accident?"

"How many stitches did you have?"

He hated the questions. Hated the thought of answering them. Hated what they made him remember.

He felt the blood drain from his face. Felt himself sway. He gripped the bench. A hand came to rest on his shoulder. Horace's hand.

"You okay, man?"

Jeremy took a breath. Nodded. The room fell silent, and in that silence everybody heard Aaron say, "Can I touch it?"

"No!" Jeremy said, pulling back. Then again, more softly, "No." He shivered at the thought and let his arm drop in an effort to hide the scar.

He was so wrapped up in thinking about himself that he barely noticed Tufan stride toward Aaron and snarl, "Creep!" Tufan jerked Aaron to his feet and shoved him, hard enough to make Aaron stumble backward until he hit the opposite wall with a thud. Some of the girls gasped, but no comforting hand reached for him as he slid down the wall to sit in a heap on the floor.

The room stayed silent until Horace offered, "My uncle has two scars. One here"—he pointed at his shoulder—"and one here." He pointed to his right buttock.

There was a burst of uncomfortable laughter.

"It's not funny," Horace said. "They're from real bullets."

The laughter stopped. Feet shuffled, eyes dropped.

"How'd he get shot?" Tufan asked. "Was it some kind of gang fight or something?"

"You don't know anything," Horace snapped. "He was in Tiananmen Square. In China. Soldiers shot him. People died there."

There was more uncomfortable shuffling, and Jeremy was surprised to hear Aaron say, "My...my father has a scar from here to here." He ran his finger down his rib cage. "I used to dream about it all the time until my counselor told me how to make the dreams stop. He said, he said, you can turn off a bad dream the same way you turn off a light. Just switch it off." Aaron used his finger to switch off an imaginary light. "Just switch it off," he said again. "I can do it now. Good thing too, 'cause my dad's scar is way uglier than yours. Yours isn't so bad. It's kind of cool, you know. Like a lightning bolt or something."

Jeremy frowned. *A lightning bolt?*

"My uncle has a scar on his hand from when he lost his thumb. It was sliced off by a machine," somebody offered, and the conversation shifted to missing body parts, until the groans from the girls in the doorway grew louder.

"What's going on here?" Mr. Collins' voice cut through the noise.

The kids looked at each other, but nobody answered until Tufan said, "Aaron wanted to touch Jeremy's leg."

"What?" Mr. Collins turned to Aaron.

"I didn't. I didn't. I didn't," Aaron said.

"Yes, you did," kids chorused.

Aaron, silenced again, began rocking his body against the cinder-block wall.

"Jeremy?" Mr. Collins said.

Jeremy looked up. He had been thinking that having a lightning bolt on his leg was kind of cool, and he had almost forgotten about Aaron wanting to touch it. "I... I think he was just curious...about...about my scar."

Mr. Collins came over to look at the red line that zigzagged down Jeremy's leg. He frowned. "With all the running and the skipping you've been doing, I assume that leg doesn't bother you a whole lot?"

Jeremy shook his head. "Not too much," he said.

Mr. Collins nodded and moved to Aaron, whose rocking had turned to banging. "Aaron. Stop. You're not in trouble. You didn't do anything wrong. Jeremy told me. You didn't do anything wrong."

With the teacher's hand on his shoulder, Aaron stopped. "Is he...is he...is he gonna die?"

Some of the kids snickered.

"Do you want to answer that?" Mr. Collins asked, turning to Jeremy.

"I hope not...," Jeremy began, but his voice caught in his throat. He began again. "I was in an accident. The doctors fixed me."

"Did they, did they stitch you up?" Aaron asked.

"Yeah. And they stapled me together. But first they put two metal plates in my leg. One here," he said, pointing at one side of his ankle, "and one here." He pointed at the opposite side.

When he looked up he noticed that the girls had drifted into the room. "The whole thing is held together with screws," he went on. "See the little bumps here, and here and here?" He pointed.

Everybody leaned forward to see.

"Man, that must've hurt," Aaron said, and for once he didn't repeat himself.

Jeremy nodded. "Yeah...but it's good now. Really," he finished, looking into Karima's concerned face. Concerned, but not grossed out.

SIXTEEN

Jeremy was happy. The assembly had been a hit, and once it was done, kids he hardly recognized said "Hi" as he passed them in the hallway and schoolyard. It was a good day. A very good day.

He came home to find Milly mopping the hallway stairs and singing a song about the moon hitting your eye and pizza. He grinned as he watched her mop dance across one step and back along another with each new line of song. The sound of his breathing must have told her she wasn't alone, because she turned abruptly.

"Hello, Jeremy," she said. "I see you've been running."

"Uh-huh. Cross-country practice. And then I jogged home with Horace."

"No wonder you look hot," Milly said. "Get yourself a glass of milk and put out some plates. Your Mom is due soon and I'm almost done."

He went into the kitchen while Milly mopped her way to the bottom of the stairs and along the hallway. "I put the kettle on," he said as she backed through the swinging kitchen door.

"Perfect." She nudged her bucket into a corner. "Tea always hits the spot."

Milly walked to the counter and dropped a couple of tea bags into the pot before she placed a plate of cookies on the table.

"Mmmm, chocolate chip. My favorite," Jeremy said, choosing one and taking a large bite.

"I thought you said peanut butter was your favorite."

"That was last week. Before I tasted these."

Milly chuckled as the front door opened and closed.

"I'm home." His mother's voice.

"We're in the kitchen," Milly called.

Jeremy put his finger to his lips and winked at Milly. She gave him a puzzled look but didn't ask any questions.

"Hello everybody," his mother said. There was a big smile on her face that vanished when she looked at Jeremy. He sat slumped in his chair, wearing a sad sorry expression.

"Oh, Jeremy…," she began. "Oh, honey…" She hurried to his side. "What happened? Was it the assembly? Did things go wrong? I knew I should have talked to your teacher."

Jeremy had meant his little act as a joke, but the pain in his mother's voice stopped him. "No," he said, and he laughed nervously. "I was kidding. Really. It was all good. Everything was great. The assembly was awesome."

"Jeremy!" her voice shook, but she laughed. "You! You're a terrible tease. You're just like your fa…" The word trailed off, but she started again. "You're just like your father," she said firmly, and then they both laughed.

"I'm dying to hear all about this assembly," Milly said, bringing the teapot to the table.

"The assembly was great," Jeremy began. He paused to collect a few stray crumbs from his plate with his finger. Once he had popped them into his mouth, he said, "Mr. Collins played music, and Aaron started by jumping up and down. He wasn't really skipping because he was holding both handles of the rope in the same hand to show what to do when you're just learning. He can't skip for beans, but he can bounce all right. Then some kids showed how to do heel-toe taps and Karima, this girl in my class, and I did some cross-overs. She learned those really fast. And at the end, we all took turns running and jumping through the long ropes. Some of the teachers even joined in. The audience loved it. They cheered." He chuckled. "City kids don't know much about skipping, so they're easy to impress."

"Did you wear your shorts?" his mother asked.

"Yeah. Everybody who skipped wore the new uniform. That was the whole point of the assembly: to show the rest of the school how good it looks."

"And?"

"Did anybody say anything? Yeah. Mostly they asked dumb questions, so I told them about the staples and the steel plates and the screws until they were really grossed out." He reached for another cookie and took a bite before he added, "Aaron said my scar looked like a lightning bolt and he wanted to touch it. I told you how weird he is."

His mother laughed. "I don't know if he's weird, but he sounds as if he's really curious."

"Yeah. He can't help it." Jeremy took another sip of milk and a bite of cookie before he went on. "So many of the kids thought skipping was cool that they asked Mr. Collins to start a skipping club when cross-country is over, and he said yes. And guess what? Even Tufan wants to join, and he used to say that skipping was only for girls."

That night Jeremy had a different dream. In this dream, dots of blood, the size of mealworm droppings, bubbled up along his scar line. Aaron appeared, saying, "Can I touch it? Can I touch it?" and his finger came closer and closer until Jeremy shouted, "No! Don't!"

"You're scared," Aaron said. He sounded sad.

Jeremy nodded.

Aaron made a quick motion with his finger, as if he were switching off a light. "Then turn it off."

"Yeah, right."

"Try it."

Jeremy raised his hand to turn off an invisible switch just as a beam of hallway light hit his face and woke him. His mother was a shadow in the doorway.

"Same dream?" she asked.

"No...No. It was nothing. Sorry."

"You okay?"

"Fine. Really."

She closed the door. He waited. When he heard her go back to her own room, he turned on his bedside lamp, shoved his quilt aside and pulled up his pajama pants to peer at his leg. The scar was there, same as ever, but there was no blood...and his bed was dry.

SEVENTEEN

Another Saturday. The morning was damp and grey and cold, with a wind that whispered of winter. The park was packed with kids. It vibrated with noise and tension.

"Okay, guys!" A teacher's voice bellowed through a megaphone. *Guys...guys...guys!* boomeranged from the trees. The boys on the starting line shifted. "Pay attention...*tention...tention...tention!*"

"We're listening," Tufan grumbled. "Start already. It's freezing out here."

"Ya got that right," Horace chimed in. He was slapping his arms across his chest. Jeremy was doing the same. It didn't help much. The October wind sliced into the tender skin at the back of his neck and behind his knees.

The teacher with the megaphone gestured to the goal posts. "There's your rabbit. Wave your hand, rabbit."

A bigger kid wearing paper bunny ears semaphored with both arms.

"Follow the rabbit," the teacher went on. "He'll lead you to the finish. ARE YOU READY?"

Jeremy toed the line. Leaned forward. Eyed the rabbit. Stood statue-still even when he felt a tap on his shoulder and heard a voice say, "Hey, Jeremy."

Aaron.

Jeremy clenched his teeth and spread his elbows to fill in the gaps between himself and his neighbors. No way was he going to let Aaron lever himself into line beside him.

Neither was Horace. "Get lost!" he growled, and to Jeremy's relief Aaron stayed back until the sound of the starter's pistol ricocheted off the trees. Jeremy launched himself forward. He was anxious to run. It was his first race since the accident, and he knew that his mother and Milly were on the sidelines watching.

There was confusion at the beginning. Runners jostled for position, trying to avoid elbows and knees and the other runners who crisscrossed in front of them.

The rabbit was way out in front, already trailed by kids who were free of the pack. For a second Jeremy thought to sprint and catch up, but he remembered

Mr. Collins' advice: "Take your time," he had said. "It's a long race. You don't want to run out of steam before the end." So he worked on finding a comfortable stride that would last him to the finish.

After a while the line spread out, and the runners were spaced like beads on a necklace, with Jeremy running behind Horace. But Horace was a smooth steady runner with longer legs, and when they came to a series of small hills, Horace climbed easily, and Jeremy fell back. Other runners passed—three, four, five—and he found himself slogging along on his own.

The path was bordered by trees and shrubbery that provided some protection from the wind. Even so, the cold seeped into his right ankle and brought on a deep, uncomfortable ache and an occasional sharp pain. He tried shifting his weight to his left foot, but that meant that he was hinking along unevenly. Four more runners passed. He clenched his teeth. Evened his stride. Tried to ignore the pain. *Suck it up, Jeremy,* he told himself. *Suck it up.*

He thought of the time when he was seven and he got a fishhook stuck in his thumb. He had cried and pulled away when his father tried to examine his hand. "There's not much choice here, Jer," his dad had said when Jeremy finally let him look. "You'll just have to suck it up."

Suck it up. Suck it up.

His father had thrust the sharp end of the hook up and through the flesh without warning. "It hurts less if you don't think about what's coming," he had said. Even so, it was a while before Jeremy allowed him to cut off the jagged barb and remove the hook. That hurt too.

He ran on. *Suck it up. Suck it up. Running is nothing compared to a fishhook*, he told himself. His arms pumped, his feet pounded a beat. *Suck it up. Suck it up. Suck it up.*

It was his mother's voice that broke the spell. "Go, Jeremy! Go!"

He heard her before he saw her jogging beside the path, keeping pace with him, cheering him on. "Way to go, Jeremy! Way to go!" she shouted until he entered the chute. Milly was waiting there, her face beaming. Horace greeted him with a high-five. The number on his paper was twenty-three. Twenty-third. Not as good as Horace who finished ninth, but still…

He gasped for air. "Keep walking," his mother told him as she draped his jacket over his shoulders. Then she leaned toward him as if she was about to give him a kiss.

"Mom," he said, his voice a warning.

She straightened, lifting her hands in pretend horror as she backed off. "Sorry," she said. "I don't know what

I was thinking." Then she laughed so happily that Milly and Horace laughed too, and Jeremy couldn't help but join in.

The last of the boy runners was still straggling in when the starter's pistol went off again. *That will be for the girls' race,* Jeremy thought.

"I'll be right back," he called over his shoulder, as he slipped his arms into his jacket and hurried back the way he had come. He would go back for Karima—to run the last stretch with her, to help her finish the way his mother had helped him.

He met two of the last boy runners coming in. They were plodding, their heads down, their breath harsh in their throats, their feet barely moving. "You're almost there," Jeremy called. "Don't stop now, you're almost there."

He was searching for a place to wait, a place with enough shrubbery to protect him from the wind, when the sight of another runner stumbling around a curve made him groan. Only one person he knew ran like a wounded duck. Aaron.

Aaron looked as if he'd been attacked by a roving mud puddle. He was caked with the stuff, and the mud on his arms and legs was reddened by the blood oozing from his knees and elbows.

"Hey, Jeremy." Aaron waved. He seemed happy enough in spite of the way he looked.

"Hey, Aaron." Jeremy tried to hide his annoyance. "Keep going. You're almost there."

But Aaron stopped. "I can't find the rabbit," he said.

"The rabbit's long gone. Just keep going and you'll get to the finish."

Aaron didn't leave.

"For crying out loud, Aaron!" Jeremy shouted. He didn't want Aaron around when Karima arrived. "Go! Go on!"

Aaron stayed.

Jeremy took a breath. "Come on," he said and he began slowly jogging beside Aaron to get him restarted. Aaron started all right, but every time Jeremy stopped, he did too. Finally, not knowing what else to do, Jeremy ran on.

The girls' rabbit and the first of the girl runners lapped them as Jeremy steered Aaron into the chute to finish dead last in the boys' race.

Seconds later Karima flashed through. She disappeared into a circle of laughing girls before he had a chance to congratulate her. He realized then that waiting for her had been a dumb idea. She'd have outrun him on the way back anyway.

Still, he couldn't help being annoyed with Aaron. *He spoils everything*, Jeremy was thinking as he joined his mother and Milly, who were talking with an older woman. That woman leaned out and grabbed Aaron when he walked by. She pulled a sweatshirt over Aaron's head and helped him put his arms into the sleeves. *His grandmother? Had to be.*

"You must be Jeremy," she said with a wide smile when he approached. "It was so nice of you to go back for Aaron."

Jeremy shook his head. "I didn't…," he said.

"It's no wonder he talks about you all the time, says you're his best friend ever. Right, Aaron?"

Jeremy felt trapped. He was sick of Aaron. Sick of Aaron telling the whole world they were friends. "We're not friends," he blurted out.

The woman's smile vanished. Milly and his mother exchanged glances. "We're not friends," he said again. "The teacher says we have to work together, but we're not friends, are we, Aaron?"

If Aaron heard, he didn't answer. He was picking off the crusty layers of drying mud and blood that matted the fine hair on his legs.

"Jeremy," his mother said, her voice filled with disapproval.

He glared at her. *I won't apologize*, he thought. *I won't. You can't make me.* But she didn't say anything else. She just looked at him and her look was...sad? Disappointed? He wasn't sure, but he couldn't face it and he turned away.

Beside him Aaron was still picking dirt from his knees, while his grandmother fussed. "Stop that," she said. "Stop that!" and she tried to pull Aaron's hands away. Then, sounding a little helpless, she turned to Milly. "I'll have to find someplace to clean him up."

"They've got wet towels at the first aid station," a new voice said, and Jeremy turned to see Karima. She smiled and gave him a little wave, but she spoke to Aaron.

"Hey, Aaron," she said. "You're a mess. Come on, I'll show you where you can get cleaned up." And to everyone's surprise Aaron followed her.

Jeremy watched them walk away. He could see Karima lean towards Aaron and say something. Whatever it was, it made Aaron laugh, and Jeremy felt a little jealous. That's where he wanted to be, walking beside Karima.

"I don't know how I'll ever get those clothes clean again," Aaron's grandmother said as she hurried to catch up.

"I should probably help," Milly said and she followed too, leaving Jeremy alone with his mother.

He glanced at her. Now that everybody was gone would she tell him he had been rude? He was ready for that. *It's wasn't my fault,* he would tell her. *I never told him I'd be his friend.*

But she didn't say anything. He heard her sigh, saw her fumble in her purse, pull out a tissue, blow her nose. "I…I have to go," she said when she was done. "My shift starts in half an hour." He nodded and watched her walk away without saying good-bye.

She didn't even try to give me a kiss, he thought. He wasn't sure if he would have objected this time.

In the distance, the starter's pistol went off again. It was followed by the roar from cheering spectators as a new race started, but for Jeremy the joy of cross-country running was over for that day.

EIGHTEEN

It was way past noon when the bus dropped the runners off at school. Jeremy was cold and tired and hungry, but he took his time getting home. He wasn't worried about facing his mother. He didn't think she'd say anything else about Aaron. She hardly ever got mad at him anymore. Not since the accident. Ever since his father died, she was careful not to upset him, so careful that her silence bothered him. For a while he had tried annoying her on purpose. He had ignored her calls to dinner and burped loudly at the table. Once, when she bought him a new shirt, he snapped, "That is so not cool." Before the accident she would have reminded him about his manners, sent him to his room or yelled at him. For sure she would have made him apologize. Now…?

Now she only frowned and looked sad. In some ways that was worse than being yelled at.

No, it wasn't his mother he was afraid to face, it was Milly.

She'd been really nice ever since they came to stay with her. Never got mad. Never shouted. Never bossed him around. But today...? Today she had looked disappointed, and he wondered what she would say.

"Hi, Milly," he said, faking cheerfulness as he walked into the kitchen.

Milly was standing behind the ironing board. He looked for one of her welcoming smiles. It didn't appear.

She did say, "Hello, Jeremy," but she didn't look at him, and he could tell from her tone that she wasn't happy.

"Is Mom home yet?"

"She'll be late. She has to make up the time she took off to see you run."

The muscles in his stomach tightened. His hunger faded.

Milly walked to the stove and brought a cup of tomato soup and a sandwich to the table for him. It looked good. It smelled good. He wrapped his fingers around the cup, enjoying the warmth, but he didn't pick up the spoon.

He watched Milly return to the ironing board and pull one of his shirts from the laundry basket. He saw her lips pinch and the lines over her nose pucker. The iron came down with a *thwack* as she pressed wrinkles out of first one sleeve, then the other, flipped the shirt and smacked the iron down again. He sighed. She was mad. He could tell.

"I should have told you that I've known Aaron's grandmother for a long time," she said.

"You mean...you're friends?"

"Yes. No. We're not close friends. We run into each other here and there. At the grocery store or the library. Like that. And we talk."

The muscles in Jeremy's stomach clenched, and his arm wrapped protectively across his middle.

"As for Aaron. Well, that boy doesn't make life easy for her."

No kidding, was on Jeremy's lips, but he knew this wasn't the time for a smart remark.

Milly finished ironing the shirt before she spoke again. "Did you know that his parents are both gone?"

Jeremy shook his head. He hadn't given Aaron's parents much thought.

"He was only two when his mother died," Milly went on. "It was some kind of cancer. The doctors gave her treatments before she knew she was pregnant. They stopped as soon as they found out, but maybe not soon enough. Some of Aaron's problems might come from that. Cancer medication and babies don't do well together."

"What…what happened to his father?"

"He took off after his wife died. He calls every so often but he hasn't come back."

"Oh…I thought he was sick or something."

"What made you think that?"

"I thought Aaron said his dad had a scar on his chest."

Milly frowned and Jeremy wasn't sure if it was because she was thinking about Aaron's father or the shirt she was folding.

Then she said, "When Aaron was little, his grandmother told him that his father left because he had a broken heart and that was something doctors couldn't fix. I suppose Aaron imagined a scar."

She pulled a tablecloth from the basket. "It can't be easy for Aaron either: a boy living alone with his grandmother."

"He's not alone. He's got a brother."

"Brother? He doesn't have a brother."

"But we saw him. On the streetcar. His name's Paul. He said he was Aaron's big brother."

"Oh, Paul. I forgot about Paul. He's with that Big Brothers, Big Sisters organization. He's a high-school student who spends time with Aaron every couple of weeks. Nice boy, but not his real brother."

Jeremy stared into the soup congealing in his cup. His shoulders sagged. "How come you're telling me now?" he asked.

"Aaron's grandmother says you're Aaron's best friend. I thought you should know."

"But...I'm not his friend," Jeremy said stubbornly. He didn't want to give in on this. "You know I've been complaining about Aaron since the first day of school. It's not my fault that he's weird. He drives *everybody* crazy. Why do *I* have to be his friend?"

Milly matched the ends of the tablecloth and folded it in half and then in half again. She ran her hands across the cloth before she looked up. "I can understand why he's a nuisance to you," she said.

"But you're making it sound like I *have* to be his friend," Jeremy said, prepared to argue.

"No..." Milly shook her head. "That's a decision only you can make." She leaned down to pull the iron's plug from the wall. "But I think it's sad, isn't it, that someone you don't like at all thinks you're the best friend he has."

She collapsed her ironing board then and carried it out of the kitchen, leaving Jeremy with a mouthful of protests and no one to hear them.

NINETEEN

On Monday Jeremy went back to school prepared to give Aaron another chance. Maybe they could be friends *some* of the time.

When Mr. Collins gave the class time to work on their mealworm projects, everything went well—for a while. He and Aaron drew a design for a maze, and when they showed it to Mr. Collins, the teacher said, "I think that experiment's worth a try."

He sent them to borrow a bin of blocks from the kindergarten and they settled on the floor at the back of the room and began building. When the maze had an outer wall and three small rooms for the mealworms to wiggle through in their search for food, Aaron began building a tower at the entrance.

Jeremy sat back on his heels. "There's no tower in the plan," he said, trying to keep his voice calm and reasonable. "Besides, we're building a maze, not a castle."

"But, but, but what if we put them in the tower first? It would give them a chance to see the maze from the air. An' then, an' then, they'd know where they have to go. Before, you know, before they enter the maze. An', an', an' the first mealworm that gets out of the tower gets a head start."

"It's an experiment, not a contest," Jeremy said, his voice not nearly as calm as before. "We're trying to find out how mealworms find food, not how they get out of towers."

"Yeah, but this will make it more interesting."

"But they'll fall. Mr. Collins said we're not supposed to do anything to hurt them, remember?" And then all his calm left him and he said, "Why can't you for once do what you're supposed to do?"

"You're not the boss of me!" Aaron crowed.

"But I'm the boss of your mealworm," Jeremy began, and then he couldn't stop. "I'm the one responsible for what you do to it and I'm not letting you drop a mealworm from your stupid tower. What if you kill it? You're such a pain!"

"You're not the boss of me!" Aaron crowed again as he added another block to his tower.

The tower, already twelve blocks high, teetered. When it steadied Aaron smiled triumphantly. "Now I just need a red block for the top," he said, rooting through the bin. "The kind that has a hole in it that looks like a bridge."

"There aren't any more," Jeremy snarled. Feeling almost pleased, he added, "I used the last one."

"Oh," said Aaron, scanning the maze. Then he reached over and plucked out the block he wanted, destroying a section of the wall Jeremy had just finished.

"Hey! Give it!" Jeremy reached to take the block back.

"Mine!" Aaron said.

"How's it going, guys?" Mr. Collins spoke softly as he squatted on the floor beside them. Jeremy's lips pinched into a tight line. He was too angry to answer.

"I made a tower," Aaron said. "So we can find out what happens when mealworms are in a high place. Like, do they jump off or do they look over the side and say, 'Uh-oh. Too high.'"

"That's quite a drop for a little creature like a mealworm," Mr. Collins pointed out. "What if your mealworm's not smart enough to stay away from the edge?"

"Then it's gonna fall."

"It certainly will. And you're its protector. So what will you do to protect it?"

"Jeremy can catch it. He's a good catcher."

Jeremy grimaced.

"What if he misses?"

"It'll hit the floor and *kapowee!*"

"Exactly."

"And he'll die?"

"Maybe. Why not pass on the tower and stick with the maze," Mr. Collins said before he walked away.

Aaron didn't say anything as he crossed his legs and started rocking.

"Let's see what happens when we put the mealworms in the maze," Jeremy said, trying to sound cheerful now that he had the teacher's support. He put a small pile of bran at the far end, took Spot from the can and placed him just inside the entrance. The mealworm didn't move. "You wanna put Darth Vader beside him?"

No answer from Aaron.

"Come on, put him in," Jeremy said, knowing he sounded like a grown-up trying to convince a kid he'd love broccoli if only he'd try some.

Aaron didn't move, so Jeremy scooped Darth Vader from his tin-can home and put him down beside Spot. Darth Vader wriggled and twisted and whipped back and forth; then he stopped too. When Jeremy nudged them, Spot barely moved, but Darth Vader wriggled to the nearest wall and stretched out beside one of the blocks.

"This is no good," Jeremy said, "What do you think?"

Aaron didn't answer.

Jeremy peered at the mealworm. Spot was longer and much fatter than he used to be. Maybe that's why he was so slow. He nudged the mealworm again, but as he did, his hand brushed a block and he was horrified to see a section of the wall collapse, burying Spot.

Jeremy's hand flashed out, but in his hurry to rescue Spot, his balance shifted, and his hand came down on a block. He felt the squish underneath.

When he lifted the block, Spot was a flat wet splotch on the floor.

My fault. My fault. I killed it. My fault. His hand went to his throat. He saw Aaron staring, his eyes large and round. Saw him frown. Saw him snatch Darth Vader from the mess on the floor and drop him into Spot's can. Saw him sweep his hand in a wide arc and shout, "*Kapowee!*" as he collapsed his tower and sent blocks sliding across the room.

"Mr. Collins," somebody called out. "Look what Aaron did."

Mr. Collins was already on his way. "It was my—," Jeremy began, but Aaron rolled on the floor and started to howl.

"Enough already," Mr. Collins said. For the first time he lost his cool and shouted, "Stop! Stop right now."

Aaron howled on. By the time he was removed from the classroom, everyone knew that a mealworm had died and everybody believed that it was Aaron who had killed it. By then Jeremy thought it was too late to tell what really happened.

It's only a mealworm, he told himself. *Just a mealworm.* But the guilt of the tiny mealworm's sudden death stayed as a heavy weight on his mind. *My fault. My fault. I killed it. My fault.*

 TWENTY

On Tuesday Aaron sat in his chair and rocked. He didn't talk, or answer questions, or do any work. Jeremy was left to finish their maze experiment on his own. It turned out to be a bust. Darth Vader refused to move even when he was nudged, and Jeremy couldn't think what to do. He was too embarrassed to ask Aaron for advice.

Wednesday and Thursday dragged. Lessons were hard to follow. When he wasn't thinking about Aaron and the mealworms, Jeremy's mind was filled with Thanksgiving and the trip home.

And then, sometime between Thursday night and Friday morning, Darth Vader disappeared. He didn't exactly vanish. He changed. Just like that. Overnight.

He was still a mealworm when Jeremy went home, but in the morning when he looked into the can, there was a little cream-colored pupa. Everybody came over to see, so Jeremy stepped back and let them look. He didn't feel any joy in the attention. It wasn't his mealworm. It was Aaron's, and Aaron was the only one who didn't come.

Mr. Collins talked about how mealworms have a life cycle just like butterflies and moths. "They go through a metamorphosis," he said, "but what comes out of the pupa is a beetle, and the beetle goes on to lay eggs that hatch out into mealworms, and so on." He showed them a circle of drawings to explain the different stages.

Aaron knew that, Jeremy thought. *He's a lot smarter than the kids in the class realize. If only…he wasn't such a pain.*

That night when sleep didn't come, Jeremy lay in bed and began counting off days on his fingers. Friday, Saturday, Sunday, Monday, Tuesday. *Five more sleeps,* he thought, remembering what his mother used to say when he was little and waiting for Christmas or his birthday. *Five more sleeps and we're going home.*

He couldn't wait to go back to Nova Scotia. He wanted to see Nana and Grampa, to walk in the woods, to climb over the rocks, to play tag with the waves. He couldn't wait to see everything. No, not everything. He didn't want to see their old house. Somebody else lived there now. Probably some other kid played in the yard. Maybe some other dog lived in the run. He wouldn't think about that.

He squirmed. He didn't want to think about Aaron either. *I should have told. I should have told.* He knew why he hadn't. It wasn't so much about what the other kids thought. It was because Mr. Collins had expected him to be responsible. *I messed up,* he thought. *Messed up again.*

On Monday Jeremy woke to the sound of rain and wind and the shock of Thomas's wet nose in his ear. Jeremy flipped onto his stomach and pulled the covers over his head. The cat bounded lightly onto his back and balanced his way down his body and along his left leg until Jeremy groaned and rolled out of bed. Another rainy Monday. *Just two more sleeps,* he comforted himself. *Just two more days of Aaron and mealworms.*

It was still raining at morning recess, so nobody was surprised when Mr. Collins said, "Have your snacks at your desk and then find a quiet activity."

What did surprise Jeremy was Karima. She looked right at him and said, "I brought a deck of Uno cards." Turning to include Horace and Tufan she asked, "Do you guys wanna play?" Jeremy saw Horace hesitate, and he heard Tufan snort. Would he say no? None of the boys ever played with the girls at recess—not outside and not in the classroom.

"Sure," Jeremy said quickly. "I like Uno." To his relief, Horace nodded and after a moment of hesitation, Tufan nodded too.

"Why not?" he said, snatching the cards from Karima's hand. "I'll deal."

Jeremy smiled, but when Karima smiled back he looked away.

He saw Aaron at the front of the room standing on his tiptoes, reaching for the ceiling. Jeremy couldn't see what he was after, but whatever it was, it was too high, and Aaron pulled over a chair and climbed up.

"Aaron," Mr. Collins' warning voice called, "get down please."

Ignoring the teacher, Aaron reached again. Then Jeremy saw the shimmery gleam of a spider's silk. As he watched, Aaron grasped the fine thread between his thumb and finger and stepped down. With the thread in his hand and the spider dangling, he walked slowly toward the back of the room.

"What's he doing?" Karima asked.

Jeremy laughed. "He's taking a spider for a walk."

"What a dweeb," Tufan said. He was dealing out cards and barely looked up. "Why doesn't he step on it?"

"Step on a spider and you'll have rain," Karima said.

"We've already got rain, haven't we?" Tufan said. "What kind of stupid superstition is that anyway?"

"I've heard that too," Horace said. "Maybe it's true."

"If you wish to live and thrive, let a spider run alive," Jeremy added, remembering something he had heard Nana say.

"You guys are all weird," Tufan said. "Play the game."

Jeremy picked up his cards. He was organizing his hand when Aaron's announcement voice interrupted them.

"Mr. Collins. Mr. Collins. Mr. Collins. The snake's gone."

Everybody saw Mr. Collins hurry to the back of the room and glance into the snake's vivarium.

"Tanisha, close the door. Now!" he called to the girl who sat closest. Then, in a softer voice, "All right, everybody. It's just a garter snake and it's probably scared. I need you to stay right where you are and look around. Tell me if you see it. It's probably hiding beside or behind or inside something. Let's find it before it gets out of the room."

"You mean it's loose in here?" Tufan said, and Jeremy was surprised to hear a tremor in Tufan's voice. A couple of girls gave little squeaking screams as if they were practicing being afraid.

"What if it's inside a desk?" somebody said, and more kids made tentative screaming noises.

"Settle down!" Mr. Collins called. Then more loudly, "Listen up!" But before he could say anything else, Aaron dove behind a box.

"Got it," he said. When he stood up, the snake was in his hands. It did not look happy. Its tail whipped around Aaron's wrist. The forked tongue flicked, tasting the air, and its head made several lunges in its search for freedom. Aaron shifted his hold with the snake's every movement until Mr. Collins took it from him and put it back into the vivarium.

"Well done, Aaron," the teacher said when he had fastened the top securely. "That was quick thinking."

Aaron smiled and took a fake formal bow that made some of the kids laugh. Karima started to clap and Jeremy joined her. The rest of the class clapped along good-naturedly. Everybody except Tufan.

"I hate snakes," he muttered. "Only an idiot like Cantwait would pick one up."

"I guess that makes Mr. Collins an idiot too," Karima snapped. Tufan's face flushed.

"Way to go," Jeremy told Aaron as he walked by, but the end-of-recess bell rang just then and Aaron didn't answer. Maybe he didn't hear.

Before the next lesson began, Aaron carried his chair back to his desk, but he didn't sit in it for long. Even before Mr. Collins was done talking, Aaron slipped to the floor, crossed his legs and began rocking.

He's so weird, Jeremy thought. *How can I be friends with someone that weird?* He sighed. *Two more sleeps*, he thought. *Two more sleeps and I'm going home.*

TWENTY-ONE

All the way to Nova Scotia, Jeremy's stomach churned and his chest was tight with tension. His mother, thinking he was nervous about flying, showed him where the barf bags were kept, just in case, but Jeremy knew that it wasn't the flight that was worrying him.

When they arrived at the airport, Grampa was waiting at the bottom of the escalator. He drove them to the farm where Nana welcomed them with smiles and tears.

Jeremy spent his days in the woods and beside the water and his evenings by the fire listening to the grown-ups talk. The time passed quickly, and then there was only one day left.

When he came downstairs on Sunday morning, he found Nana's kitchen filled with the promising smells of the Thanksgiving dinner to come: apples and cinnamon, onions, sage and sausage. Jeremy took a deep breath and looked around. He watched Nana tossing spoonfuls of spices into a bowl of stuffing bread while his mother stirred the cranberry sauce.

"Buddy and I are headin' out," Grampa shouted from the back hall. "Anybody else comin'?"

"Me," Jeremy called. He jumped up, spooning the last bit of oatmeal into his mouth as he carried the bowl to the sink.

"Take your time. He'll wait," Nana said. Then louder, so Grampa could hear, "You're gonna give this boy an ulcer the way you're rushing him around."

"Stop fussin', woman," Grampa called back. "He's got Williamson genes. Not one of us ever had the ulcer."

"That man!" Nana grumbled. "Doesn't he always have to have the last word."

The *nick* of the latch as the door shut was like a starting pistol to Jeremy. He raced to put on his shoes, and seconds later he was outside with his jacket in hand, pretending he hadn't heard his mother shout, "Brush your teeth."

Grampa was standing near the front of the house, lighting his pipe. "It's a right good day," he said, shielding a match flame against the wind as he puffed.

"Sure is," Jeremy said, slipping into his jacket. It was cold. The wind wasn't strong, but it carried a bite.

Grampa whistled one sharp blast, and Buddy appeared from behind the barn and walked over to join them. He was breathing hard, his red tongue hanging, his tail waving a quiet welcome. The dog leaned his full weight into Grampa, who stood straight and solid, supporting the old dog's weight.

"Ya tired yourself out again, didn't ya?" Grampa said as he leaned down. He buried his hands deep in the shaggy fur around Buddy's neck to give him a good scratch. "One of these days, you'll surely realize you're too old to be chasin' rabbits."

Jeremy liked walking with his grandfather. Grampa was a silent walker. He talked plenty at home, but when he was outside he hardly spoke at all. You could think your own thoughts when you walked with Grampa.

Their walk took them down and away from the house. The path here had two ruts made by the tractor's wheels and a higher part in the middle where the grass and the weeds and the wildflowers grew. On one side Jeremy could see the farm woodlot filled with pines and birches and a ground cover of brown-fingered ferns, on the other side, the sea, its waves rolling silently until they broke against the rocks that lined the shore.

This is nothing like home, he thought, remembering the distant wail of sirens, the painful screech of streetcar wheels on steel tracks, the cars and people and... He stopped, sucking a mouthful of air in through his teeth. Home? All the time he was in Toronto, he had thought that home was here. Now he realized that Milly's comforting presence and Thomas's rumbling purr made the Toronto house feel like home too. Was it possible to have two homes?

He looked up to find Grampa waiting, his eyes deep and dark and curious. Jeremy looked away, pretending interest in a dew-covered spider web. He didn't think he had words to explain this new feeling, so he stayed silent.

The path narrowed until they reached the clearing in front of the old fish house where Grampa stored his boat and fishing gear. Beside that was an open patch of grass, dotted with goldenrod and the flat-topped white flowers Nana called Queen Anne's Lace. The spot was sheltered from the wind and warmed by the sun. A low wooden bench sat in this space, and Jeremy watched his grandfather walk over and settle there. Buddy dropped to the ground beside him, so Jeremy followed and sat down too. For a while they were silent, staring at a rock that jutted from the sea like the nose of a whale, and the swirling patterns made by the waves flowing in from the sea.

"Grampa?" Jeremy finally said, "Did you ever have...?" He stopped. Started again. "Did you ever know somebody who wanted to be your friend, and you didn't want to be their friend back?"

Grampa banged out the tobacco in his pipe, took out his pouch and refilled it with great care before he said, "You got anybody particular in mind?"

"There's this kid in my class in the city," Jeremy began. "His name's Aaron. He's one of those guys that never knows when to be quiet, so he's always talking. The other kids call him Aaron Cantwait. That's kind of mean, I guess, but he's such a pain you can't even feel sorry for him. He bugs everybody. Even the teacher."

Jeremy stopped in case his grandfather might want to say something, but when he didn't he went on.

"And the other thing about Aaron is that he's kind of a klutz. He can't catch or throw. He can't do anything, so nobody ever wants him on their team. And you should see him run!" He chuckled at the memory of Aaron's duck-run across the gym.

"Anything good about this fellow?" Grampa asked.

"I guess," Jeremy began, wishing that he could say, *No, there's nothing good about him. Not one single thing*. But he felt that he had to be fair. "He's kinda smart about some stuff. He knows about mealworms and darkling beetles and snakes."

Grampa nodded to show that he had heard.

"And he was nice to me the day everybody saw my scar for the first time. I was kinda worried about what they'd say. I thought they might think it was really ugly and everybody would make fun of me. But Aaron said it looked like a lightning bolt."

When Grampa still didn't say anything Jeremy took a deep breath and told him the one thing he hadn't told anyone yet. "One day we made this maze for our mealworms. It collapsed, and my mealworm was smushed, but Aaron didn't tell that it was my fault. He took the blame and he gave me his mealworm and now he doesn't have one of his own."

Grampa nodded again to show that he had heard. He peered at his pipe. "Padric Sullivan comes to mind," he said. He struck a match, relit the tobacco and puffed a few times before he went on. "The two of us went up the coast together one winter where we had jobs lined up in a lumber camp. That was…oh, must be fifty-five, sixty years ago now. We were just young fellows at the time. Neither one of us wanted to stay in school and that was our first job away." He stopped talking to puff on his pipe before he went on.

"I wasn't looking forward to travelin' with Padric. We weren't friends; just happened that we both needed work and ended up heading for the same place. Padric

talked the whole way. Had big plans, big ideas of seeing
the world, maybe taking flying lessons, joining the army
and going off to Korea. Talked on and on. Most of it
nonsense. Didn't know that ears need a rest every so
often. By the time we got to the lumber camp, I was right
tired of the sound of his voice." Grampa chuckled and
shook his head as if he could still hear Padric's voice.

"I remember there were three empty bunks left
when we got there, two together and one at the far end
of the bunkhouse. I headed for the one at the far end.
Settled in there, happy to be on my own.

"Turned out the crew boss sent men out in pairs,
and guess who he paired me up with? Padric, of course.
By jiminy, I was mad. Wouldn't talk to him for three days
'less it had somethin' to do with the job. And that job
was hard. It was cold in the woods, and the other men
were all older than us. Turned out that we were paired
up because none of them wanted new boys anywhere
near where they were working."

Jeremy was surprised. It was hard to believe that his
grandfather had ever had a hard time with anything.

"On the fourth day," Grampa continued, "a storm
moved in. The sky was gray in the morning when we
left the camp, and it only got grayer. The wind came up,
and even in the woods with all those trees, it blew so
hard it hurt. We worked, not even stopping for lunch,

because we worried the horses might cool down and freeze if they stopped moving. 'Let's head back,' Padric said a couple of times, but I wouldn't answer him, so he kept working too.

"Now the thing of it was that I wanted to go back, but I was waiting for him to lead the way, thinking that once he went, I would follow. But he didn't go, and I was too mule-headed to go first.

"We finished our shift that day and I led the horses back to the camp, the snow so deep they had a hard time of it. Padric had a hard time too. I could see that his feet hurt, and I felt a little sorry for him so I didn't say anything when he sat on the sled on the way back. As it turned out it was the worst thing he could'a done. The cold froze his toes. They had to take him to town and the doc lopped off two on one foot and one on the other."

Grampa stopped talking. When Jeremy glanced at him, he saw tight lips and a dampness at the corner of his eyes. Grampa pulled a handkerchief out of a pocket and blew his nose before he went on.

"Boss called Padric a fool for not coming in sooner, but Padric never once blamed me for staying out in the storm. Told me later he was afraid to leave me in the woods. Worried I might die of cold. Said he didn't want to lose his best buddy."

"Were you friends after that?" Jeremy asked.

"For life. Padric decided to go back to school the next year, so I went along." He chuckled. "After working in the woods, school didn't seem so hard or so boring anymore. If it weren't for Padric, I never would have finished high school."

"What happened to him?"

"There's a lot of jobs you can't do when you're missin' toes, but it turned out that doctoring wasn't one of them."

"He became a doctor?"

Grampa nodded. "A darn good one." He smiled. "And when he was done with all his schoolin', he married my little sister and became your mother's favorite uncle."

"You mean Uncle Pat?"

"That's the one."

Buddy stood up and gave himself a shake. "You ready to head back?" Grampa asked.

Jeremy nodded.

They walked in silence for a while before Grampa said, "I dunno if that answers your question. I suppose there are some things in life you have to decide for yourself."

Jeremy's shoulders sagged just a little. Then he sighed. "I guess I knew that."

TWENTY-TWO

As Jeremy rounded the corner of the house, he heard Nana say, "There can't be too many days like this left in the year."

He looked up. She was alone on the bench that ran across the back of the porch. Her eyes were closed, her face turned to the sun. A leaf, streaked yellow and brown, floated down and settled unnoticed on her shoulder. Through the window behind her came the clanking sounds of pans and the *swoosh* of water running into the sink.

"Leave it for now, Carol," she called. "Come outside and enjoy this sunshine. We'll tidy up later. The dishes can wait."

Jeremy reached the porch steps just as his mother came through the door. She was drying her hands on a dish towel. "That's the potatoes all peeled and ready," she said. "We can put them on when the turkey's almost done."

"Where'd you leave Grampa?" she asked when she saw Jeremy.

"He went to get something from the shed. Said he'd be right in."

Nana smiled and patted the seat on the bench beside her. "Come. Sit," she said to his mother.

"Actually, I was thinking of driving over to our old house. Papa told me they have an Apples For Sale sign out, and I'd love to get some. You used to love those apples, Jeremy. Especially the ones from the tree by the side of the house. Remember? You wanna come?"

No! The word screamed in Jeremy's head. *No! No!* He looked up. Was he shouting? He saw Nana hoist herself from the bench.

"Great idea," she said. "I'll just check on that bird and change my shoes." Jeremy saw her walk through the door before he collapsed to the porch steps.

"Jeremy?" his mother said. "Jeremy? What's wrong? Are you all right?" She hurried down to him. "Are you sick? What's wrong?"

"I can't…," he started. "Don't make me." A pain, sharp and hard, flashed behind his eyes. And then he couldn't stop the memory: the motorcycle roaring. The sudden stop. His arms and legs spread-eagled as he flew, hands reaching toward the road and the rocks. Water and blood patterning his visor. He heard himself rasp, "Daddy? Daddy! It hurts!"

Heard Henry's pain-filled yips and saw the dog on the road, his head between his paws. "Henry?"

Henry's head lifted. He whined. Struggled to rise. Then he whimpered and dropped.

"Daddy!" Where was his father? "Daddy?" There. Beside the motorcycle, his head turned in an impossible direction.

"Jeremy?" His mother's voice cut through the nightmare images.

"No," he groaned. He shook his head and closed his eyes, hoping the pictures would go away, but they replayed behind his eyelids. He couldn't stop seeing them. Couldn't turn off the sound of the motorcycle's drone or Henry's whimpers.

Why now? He clutched his stomach and gasped. A new wave of pain spread through his body. He heaved and threw up. Once, then again and again, until there was nothing left. Still his body heaved.

He felt his mother's hands. One, firm and warm, holding his forehead, the other rubbing his back.

"I didn't. I didn't mean it," he sobbed. "I didn't mean it."

"It's okay, baby," she said. "It's okay. People throw up. It happens."

"No...," he tried to speak, but she wouldn't let him go on.

"Just breathe," she said, "just breathe." Her hands never let go.

TWENTY-THREE

Later, when he was washed and dressed again, he sat on the living-room couch bundled in one of Nana's afghans. He was rocking. *Like Aaron,* he thought. *Just like Aaron.* He willed himself to stop, but his body wouldn't cooperate.

Nana and his mother were seated on either side of him, Grampa on the chair opposite. Their faces mirrored their concern. He had to tell. He wanted to tell. *They'll hate me,* he thought. But he couldn't keep his secret. Not anymore.

"I was...I was so excited to ride on the motorcycle. I knew you didn't want me to." He glanced at his mother. "But..." He shrugged. "I held on to Dad's middle the way he told me, and I leaned when we turned onto the road.

I did everything he said. After we rounded the curve I looked back. I was gonna wave…but you were gone."

"I was mad at your father," she whispered. "I went inside because I couldn't stand to see you leave."

"That's when I saw Henry," Jeremy went on. "He was cutting across the field. You know how fast he could run. He looked like he was flying. I called out to Dad, but he didn't hear. I shouted. I guess he couldn't hear me over the noise of the engine. I pounded on his shoulder, but by that time Henry was beside us. Dad swerved. We hit…I don't know what we hit." His voice cracked, and he coughed to clear his throat. "We stopped just like that." His right hand smacked against the left. "And I went flying."

"Oh, Jeremy." His mother reached for his hands, but he shook her away, knowing what he still had to tell.

"It was my fault," he said. "Don't you see? It was… my fault."

"No!" His mother wrapped her arms around his shoulders. "How could it have been your fault?"

"I…I didn't close the latch on the dog run." The words spilled out. "I must not have closed it. That's how Henry got out. It was my fault that Daddy died." Then in a whisper, "It's okay if you hate me."

It wasn't until the second time she spoke that Jeremy heard his mother's words. "You're wrong," she was saying. "Can you hear me? Listen to me! You're wrong!"

He looked up, tears flooding his eyes.

"The gate was locked," she said firmly when she had his attention. "Officer McKendrick checked after the accident. It was the wire mesh that gave way. You know how Henry always hurled himself against the fence. The staples gave way, and he squeezed through. That's how he got out. It wasn't your fault. It was *not your fault*," she said, as if the repetition would make her words more true.

Jeremy searched her face, but her eyes never wavered.

"It was not your fault," she said again. "I should have told you. I wanted to tell you everything, but every time I tried talking about the accident, I got too upset. I kept crying. I couldn't help it. And every time I cried you got upset too…and you had those terrible dreams…

"I should have guessed that you were blaming yourself. It's not your fault," she said for the fourth time. "Even if…" She wiped her eyes. "Even if…I could never hate you Jeremy. Never."

TWENTY-FOUR

They were in the truck on their way to the airport when Jeremy said, "Do we have time to pick up apples?"

Grampa and his mother exchanged glances. "You sure about that?" his mother asked.

"Yeah. I told Milly our apples were the best. If she doesn't taste them, how will she know?"

"One road's as good as another," Grampa said. He turned left at the next corner and started along the road that ran past their old house.

Jeremy sat, his chin high, his eyes straight ahead, until he saw the Apples For Sale sign, and he glanced to the left in time to see a flash of blue roof between the trees. Home?

Grampa turned the truck into the lane and stopped beside the house. It looked the same—but different.

A woman came out and greeted them. She led Grampa and his mother to the back where the apple shed was. Jeremy stayed in the driveway and looked around. The dog run was gone, replaced by a long, lower shelter that he recognized as a chicken coop.

Chickens, he thought. *No dog.*

An unexpected voice made him jump. "I know you," the voice said. "You're Jeremy."

He turned to see a small girl on the other side of the screen door. He knew her from somewhere. School maybe?

"You're Joanne," he said.

"I know," said the girl, and she came outside to stand beside him. "I'm in grade one."

Jeremy smiled. "Yeah. I remember."

She was dressed in blue corduroy overalls that had a turkey and some corn sheaves embroidered on the bib.

"You have chickens," Jeremy said.

"I know," said the girl. "You wanna see?" She was already walking toward the henhouse.

When she opened the door for him he bent to look inside. The henhouse held about a dozen young chickens, all past the cute chick stage, but bits of yellow down still stuck out in patches between their sprouting feathers.

"Your chickens are teenagers," Jeremy said.

"I know," said the girl.

He closed the henhouse door. "There used to be a dog run here," he said, and then stifled the urge to laugh when she said, "I know."

"It died," she said. "You wanna see?"

Jeremy frowned. "See what?"

She took his hand and led him to the old apple tree beside the house. His tree.

"There," she said, pointing to a large rock. "Daddy says he's under there."

"The dog?"

"Your dog."

For a long moment Jeremy stared at the gray boulder. Henry's stone.

The sound of his mother's voice made him jump. "You found it," she said.

He turned to see her standing with legs braced, as if she was fighting a wind. Her arms were wrapped protectively around a bag of apples. Grampa stood beside her.

"He died that first night," she said. "You were in the hospital."

"Yeah."

"I was...I should have told you."

"I knew. I didn't want to hear."

She took a deep breath, and when Jeremy didn't say anything else she went on. "Grampa buried him. We thought that was a good place."

Jeremy nodded.

"You didn't ask...I didn't know...I was..."

"His name was Henry," the little girl interrupted.

"I know," said Jeremy, but he was answering his mother.

On the flight home, Jeremy talked about his father for the first time since the accident. "You know what I remember?" he began. He went on to tell his mother about sharing an apple; about finding Henry and how he thought the pups were a bear; how he had a fish-hook stuck in his thumb; how much he loved camping. He talked on and on while his mother listened. She had heard all the stories before, but it didn't matter. She was happy to hear Jeremy share them again.

When they walked through the door of Milly's house, he called, "We're home," and Milly came from the kitchen and welcomed them back with a hug. This time Jeremy didn't mind. In fact, he hugged Milly back before they gave her the bag of apples.

"I guess I'm making pies tomorrow," she said with a smile. "Do you want a plain or crumble topping?"

"Make them the way Fred liked them," Jeremy said. "I think that's the kind my dad liked too."

At bedtime he was tired and his bed seemed to welcome him. He fell asleep easily and slept well—until the dream returned. The good part was better than ever. He watched his father pull off the helmet and smile. He felt the wind from the sea, smelled the leather of his father's jacket and the nose-biting sting of gasoline. He heard the roar of the motorcycle's engine as it kicked in, and his body vibrated with happiness—until the bad part started. He could feel it in the rhythm of his heart, which began a painful drumming.

No, he protested. *I don't want to see. I don't want to see.* He covered his eyes, determined not to look.

"You don't have to," a voice said.

"What?" Jeremy was confused. Aaron? Why was Aaron in his dream again?

Aaron made one of his gargoyle faces. "Just, just turn it off," he said, and he made a flicking motion, as if he were turning off a light.

Jeremy, desperate to escape the dream images, reached with his finger and tried to turn them off. They didn't stop. The motorcycle roared on and on.

Aaron's face appeared again. Jeremy couldn't hear him over the roar, but he saw Aaron mouthing the words, "Turn…it…off!"

He woke with a start, gasping, his heart beating double time, but when he checked, his bed was dry.

He waited, listening for his mother. She didn't come. *I didn't scream*, he thought, and he turned and settled back to sleep. When he woke it was morning, and his room was filled with sunshine.

TWENTY-FIVE

His mother was already buttoning her coat when Jeremy came downstairs for breakfast. "Have to run," she said. "I've got an early class." She gave him a quick peck on the cheek. "Bye, Milly," she called, and she was gone.

Milly was by the window when Jeremy walked into the kitchen.

"It's a perfect apple pie day," she said with a smile.

He came to stand beside her, and they looked out, admiring the reds and yellows and greens of the autumn garden. The sun was bright, the sky a brilliant shade of blue. *It does look perfect*, Jeremy thought. *It feels perfect too*. And he was happy until he remembered that this was the day he was going to make things right with Aaron. Then it didn't seem quite as golden.

Milly interrupted his thoughts. "I forgot to tell you," she said. "Aaron came around looking for you while you were in Nova Scotia."

"Aaron?" Was she reading his mind?

"He didn't seem to know that you'd be away for Thanksgiving."

"Yeah. I...I didn't tell anybody. I..." He sighed, remembering how worried he had been about the trip home. Now he felt a little silly about keeping everything a secret.

"You didn't want to answer questions?"

"Yeah." He grinned. Milly seemed to understand all the things he couldn't put into words. "What did Aaron want?"

"Oh, Aaron." She hesitated. "He was funny. He was bouncing up and down so much he could hardly talk. Said he had good news."

Jeremy felt her study his face as she spoke. "His father phoned and talked to him. I didn't get all the details because he was bubbling with excitement, but he said his dad would be coming back to Toronto sometime before Christmas." She paused again. "I thought I should tell you. I'm sure you'll hear all about it at school. It doesn't seem like a secret he'd be able to keep."

An unexpectedly sharp stab of envy hit Jeremy, and all the good feelings of the morning oozed from his body. There was nothing about Aaron he had ever envied. Nothing. Until now. But now he wished he had a father who could phone, a father who would be home for Christmas. He realized he missed his dad so much that it hurt with a deep painful ache that made him want to cry. *It hurts. It hurts. It hurts,* he thought. The words rang in his head as he fought back his tears.

There was a long silence in the kitchen. When he finally looked up, he realized Milly was still watching. From the look on her face, he knew she understood.

"It's always a surprise when it hits you," she said softly. "And it doesn't go away. Not completely. But after a while, it doesn't hurt nearly as much. Not nearly as much. You'll see."

By the time he arrived at school, it was almost time for the bell. Kids were milling about, talking. They sounded excited. A long weekend always made the Tuesday back feel like a new beginning. He looked around until he spotted Horace standing with Karima and Tufan and some other kids from the class. They were in a sort of huddle around Aaron, who was talking, his hands and feet dancing with the excitement of his words. Jeremy figured he knew what that was all about, but he went to join them anyway.

"…and he said he has a surprise for me," he heard Aaron say as he joined the group.

"Therapy," Tufan said, and he snickered. "He's heard all about you and he's going to sign you up for therapy."

The excitement drained from Aaron's face. His hands fell to his side.

"That's just mean," Karima scolded.

"What? How is that mean? You don't think his dad's gonna freak when he sees him? He's either gonna spring for therapy sessions, or he's gonna disappear all over again."

"Is not! Is not! Is not!" Aaron said, his words getting louder with each repetition. "He's coming back to stay! He said! He said!"

"Ya, well, my old man said he'd get me a skateboard and a bicycle, but that never happened. Fathers promise all kinds of things. It's not like they ever mean it."

"My dad always kept his promises," Jeremy said, looking right at Aaron. "Probably your dad will too."

"Yeah," Aaron said, his voice quiet now.

Tufan turned to Jeremy, and in a voice filled with sarcasm he snarled, "So your dad's perfect. Lucky you. What's he promised you lately?"

"Nothing," Jeremy said. Then he added the words he hadn't been able to say before. "My dad's dead."

The circle was silent then. Not even Tufan had a smart answer for that.

There were whispers in the classroom. Jeremy heard. He figured they were either about Aaron's dad or his own. Sometimes he felt that somebody was watching him, but when he looked up that person always looked away fast. It was as if they wanted to ask a question, or say something, but didn't know the words.

Other than that, the day wasn't too bad. Aaron sat in his chair. He did his work and hardly rocked at all. Mr. Collins noticed that there was something going on. "It's very quiet in here today," he said. "Is everybody in a turkey coma?" People chuckled, but the silence stayed.

During science, Mr. Collins told them that each set of partners would have to prepare a mealworm presentation. "You'll get planning time in class," he went on to say, "but most of the work will be done on your own."

Jeremy took a deep breath and raised his hand. He knew what he still had to do and he figured this was as good a time as any.

"Jeremy?"

"Mr. Collins. There's something I should have told before—about our mealworms," he began. He went on to explain how Spot had died, and how he was to blame, not Aaron. Once everything was told, it didn't seem so bad. Mr. Collins asked Aaron if he was willing to shake hands and Aaron said yes. When Jeremy sat down again, Karima smiled at him, and he felt washed clean, like the sand on a warm beach the morning after a high tide.

After school Jeremy walked into the gym for skipping-team practice. The room echoed with voices chanting, "Jump! Jump! Jump!"

Karima and another girl were turning a long rope for Aaron, who was skipping—or trying to. Every jump he made was higher than it needed to be. As he rose, he lifted his arms and opened his eyes and even his mouth. His knees buckled with each landing, but he looked happy.

"I'm skipping," he called when he saw Jeremy, and then he tripped.

Jeremy was surprised to hear Karima say, "That was twenty-four, Aaron. You made twenty-four jumps this time. Way to go." Then she turned to Jeremy. "You wanna help?"

"I guess," he said, and when the other girl held out her end of the rope, he took it. "Okay," he said to Aaron, "let's see if you can do it again. Only this time, try standing straighter, and remember, the rope's skinny so you don't have to jump so high."

Jeremy and Karima began to turn, and Aaron jumped. When he made it all the way to forty-six, Karima clapped for him, and Aaron was so happy he laughed out loud.

The practice session went fast. Toward the end, other kids came over and started counting along. "Seventy-two, seventy-three, seventy-four…"

"Keep going," Karima called, urging Aaron on.

"Eighty-seven, eighty-eight, eighty-nine…" The voices around them rose with excitement, and Aaron's face glowed.

Jeremy knew how important it was to turn the rope well, so his eyes stayed focused on Aaron's feet.

"Ninety-six, ninety-seven…"

He didn't see the body that came hurtling toward them until Tufan was in the middle of the rope, jumping beside Aaron.

Jeremy's first instinct was to pull back and trip Tufan, but he didn't. "Pay attention," he warned Aaron as he bent low to slip the rope under both pairs of feet, once, then again, and again.

"Ninety-eight, ninety-nine…" The gathered voices rose as they counted. "One hundred!" There was a great cheer and a lot of clapping.

Aaron raised his arms in victory. "I jumped!" he shouted. "I jumped all the way to one hundred," and he ran celebratory circles around the gym.

His happiness was infectious, and other kids started running with him. "You did it! You did it!" Karima said again and again, and Jeremy couldn't help smiling. They all looked so happy.

That day Jeremy walked Karima home. She lived up past Gerrard Street, so he went out of his way but he didn't mind. He didn't mind one bit.

"You know," she said as they walked, "with a little patience and practice, Aaron could learn to do all kinds of stuff."

"Yeah." Jeremy laughed. "With a *lot* of patience and practice, he probably can."

TWENTY-SIX

In the second week of November, everybody was ready for their mealworm presentations. Jeremy was nervous. He hated the idea of standing in front of the class, talking, and he slumped in his chair when Mr. Collins asked for volunteers. He should have known that Aaron's hand would shoot up.

No-o-o! Jeremy wanted to wail when he saw, but it was too late. Mr. Collins was already smiling. "All right, Aaron. You and Jeremy can go first," he said, and Jeremy had no choice but to walk to the front of the room where they stood beside each other. He felt awkward, but Aaron grinned and took an enormous bow.

"We did four mealworm experiments," he began in his announcement voice. **"And this is what we found out."**

"No need to shout," the teacher said softly. "We can hear."

Aaron went on more quietly. "Our mealworms ate bran and apples and pears. They ate potato peels and carrots and all the kinds of cereal we brought in. They even ate tunnels through wet paper towels. We were gonna look for a dead mouse to see if they would eat that, but we couldn't find one."

There were groans from the class, and Aaron broke into one of his hyena laughs that stopped when Jeremy nudged him. Aaron glanced at Mr. Collins, took a breath and went on.

"We proved that mealworms like dark colors better than light colors, and they like to hide. Every time we put them in our maze they stayed beside the wall. And, and, and…" His voice rose in excitement.

Jeremy nudged him again. Aaron took another breath and continued at a slower pace. "And they don't travel very fast, but they get around. Mostly at night. We put them into a paper cup and we found out that they can use the claws on the ends of their legs and climb up. They're not as good at climbing down. They fall." He grinned and crossed his eyes as he stepped back.

Some of the kids laughed again, but Jeremy ignored them and went right into his part of the report.

"Aaron's brother, Paul, took us to the museum," he began. "We found out lots of stuff about mealworms there. Like Mr. Collins told us, mealworms aren't really worms, they're the larvae of darkling beetles. They wear their skeleton on the outside like a suit of armor, but it's not really strong and it can be squished pretty easy."

"Yeah! That's how Spot became 'The Blob,'" Tufan called out. Everybody laughed again. Even Jeremy grinned. He was relieved that he had told the truth about Spot. Now it wasn't a big deal anymore.

He waited for the class to be quiet. "When mealworms grow, they have to shed their skin until they're big enough to turn into pupae. We think the reason we didn't see so many skins is, probably the mealworms ate them. Oh, and the pupa hardly moves at all unless you poke it, and then it sort of pulses from inside.

"We used our notes and the stuff we learned from our experiments to make this science diary." He held up their booklet labeled *The Mealworm Diaries*. "We took turns writing the words and drawing the pictures." Then he added, "I found out that everything I learned about mealworms was something that Aaron already knew. He knows more than anybody about science."

"You've just said a mouthful," Mr. Collins said, and the class clapped. Aaron grinned and bowed and motioned for the kids to clap some more.

That afternoon Jeremy came home to find his mother standing at the kitchen table peeling potatoes. "You're home," he said.

"Finished my first exam. Only three more to go." She grimaced. "I thought I'd give myself a break and do something besides read. How was your day?"

"Great. We did our mealworm presentation first because Aaron volunteered us. I was nervous, but once we were done, I was glad it was over with. Aaron hardly repeated himself. He wasn't even too silly."

"All that practice paid off, I guess."

"Yeah. It was good that Paul helped. Aaron listens to him."

"Seems to me that when I heard you practicing in the living room, he listened to you a fair bit too."

Jeremy flushed. His mother was right. Talking to Aaron was getting easier.

"Is this good news I hear?" Milly said, coming up from the basement. She placed a basket of laundry on a chair and walked to the cupboard.

"Yeah. We finished our mealworm presentation today."

"So what happens now?" Milly asked.

"Now?"

"Well, you and Aaron spent a good deal of time together for this project. Just wondering if that'll continue."

"Continue!" Jeremy put his head in his hands and rolled his eyes. "You think I still want to hang around with Aaron now that we're finally done with mealworms!"

"Jeremy!" His mother's voice cut in.

"What? The kid's been a total pain in the backside, and that's one of the nicest things I can say about him."

He stopped, enjoying the startled expressions on the faces of Milly and his mother, before he went on to say, "Aaron and I won't be hanging around much anymore... until tonight, when we're going to the community center to play floor hockey with Horace and a bunch of other guys, and next week, when we start the unit on outer space. Did I tell you that Aaron and I are going to be partners again? We figured we might as well, now that we're sort of used to each other."

"Jeremy!" Milly shook her head and laughed. When his mother joined in, Jeremy laughed too—a warm, loose, easy laugh. *I sound just like Dad,* he thought. *Just like Dad.* And he laughed again.

ACKNOWLEDGMENTS

More than anybody, I owe thanks to Peter Carver, who introduced me to the world of children's writing. He was there for Jeremy's birth in a short story, and he encouraged me to expand that story into a novel. Along the way I was given invaluable advice from the wise and talented members of Peter's writing classes in Toronto and Port Joli.

Special thanks go to Kathy Stinson for her feedback on an early draft of the work; to Chery Rainfield for invaluable advice; to Connie Hubbarde for being my first reader; and to my editor, Sarah Harvey, for taking a chance on a new writer and patiently allowing my story to grow.

I thank Joanne Taylor for giving Jeremy's grampa his voice, Sylvo Frank for telling me how to turn off bad dreams, Glenna Storie for "counting sleeps" and Richard Ungar for his wise counsel.

I'm grateful, also, to the Toronto Arts Council. Their recognition and support allowed me to experience, firsthand, the Nova Scotia world that Jeremy called home.

ANNA KERZ loves stories that touch the heart and tickle the funny bone. Now that she's retired from teaching, she fills her time by working as a storyteller, telling tales to audiences of all ages, and by writing books for children. She lives in Scarborough, Ontario. *The Mealworm Diaries* is her first published novel.